A novel by
BARBARA WERSBA

Wonderful Me

May.16,1991
YA0450
C.J2

Published by
Dell Publishing
a division of
Bantam Doubleday Dell Publishing Group, Inc.
666 Fifth Avenue
New York, New York 10103

ISBN: 0-440-20883-1

RL: 5.9

Reprinted by arrangement with Harper & Row Junior Books

Printed in the United States of America

June 1991

10 9 8 7 6 5 4 3 2 1

RAD

Wonderful Me

1

The title of this story is a joke. Because I have never in my life thought that I was wonderful. A boy I was in love with once told me that I was—and for a while I believed him—but basically what you get when you look at me is a short plump teenager who is rather a klutz. My nose is too big, my eyes are too small, my voice resembles Woody Allen's, and my name is not glamorous. I should have been born with a name like Francesca Cunningham or Dawn Blackwell—something that would have been an advantage—but my name is Heidi Rosenbloom. I am sixteen and a half, I live in New York City, and the summer I am going to tell you about was the craziest summer of my life.

To begin with, my mother Shirley, who is divorced from my father, had started dating a foot doctor named Dr. Eisenberg. She had found him through a friend of hers who said that Dr. Eisenberg was painless. His procedures, I mean. She had some corns on her toes, appreciated the fact that Dr. Eisenberg's address was on Park Avenue, and went to him for treatment. He cured her corns and two weeks later they were dating. It was a shock to me.

However. You have to understand that Shirley had been divorced for three years, that most of her social life was spent with other women, and that she simply was not made for such an arrangement. To Shirley, one was born female to attract a male, and that was that. Because where could a woman *go* without a man? What could a woman *do* without a man? And what was the point of being attractive if not for the pleasure of a man? As far as my mother was concerned, a single woman had no place in the world—and so after three years of shopping excursions with other women, and volunteer work at the Red Cross, and weekend trips with her best friend Bobo Lewis, and ladies' luncheons at the Four Seasons—after all this my mother was determined to have a beau. Of course, the idea of her doing anything more intimate with Dr. Eisenberg than going to Broadway musicals and Japanese restaurants turned me to stone—because he was truly terrible—but I tried not to think about that part. I tried to be glad for her.

My mother is small and dark and pretty—and

resembles Joan Bennett in old movies on television. The only man she ever loved in her life was my father, Leonard, and so when he left her for an affair with a person named Jane Anne Mosley, she was devastated. Poor Daddy. His affair did not last, but his estrangement from Shirley did, so that eventually he went to live in a tiny apartment in Greenwich Village. Mom and I stayed in the big apartment in the East 80's, and Leonard came over on birthdays and holidays.

Unlike my mother, who had grown up in comfort in Westchester, my father came from poor people and had left school to start work at fifteen. Now in his late forties, he was a big success—he owns a jewelry business on West 47th Street—but he had a lot of resentment toward my mother, who, he said, was bleeding him dry. Part of the divorce settlement was that Leonard pay alimony plus Shirley's medical bills, and he was bitter about it. You would think that a new man in Shirley's life—one who might marry her and take the burden off him—would have thrilled him. But not at all. He was incredibly jealous.

What a mistake! My mentioning Dr. Eisenberg, I mean. Because from the moment I did, Leonard started asking me questions. I see him every Saturday for lunch, and all of a sudden our only topic of conversation was Dr. Eisenberg—or, El Creepo, as I called him in the privacy of my mind. Where, Leonard wanted to know, did Dr. Eisenberg take my mother? Did she come home very late these nights? And what about his weekend house on Long Island? Did Shirley ever go there with him? Did he give her presents? And if it was true that Dr. Eisenberg was a widower, when had his wife died? God! It was like going out to lunch with J. Edgar Hoover. All of which was crazy, since Leonard had been the one to break up the marriage in the first place.

There he would sit, smoking cigarette after ciga-rette—and drinking his third martini—while I would sit slumped over a Coke, surreptitiously glancing at my watch. Not that I don't love Leonard. He is a good person, and a very good dad, but his obsession with Dr. Eisenberg was beginning to get me down. Just for the record here, my father has steel-gray hair and bright green eyes. His clothes are pure Brooks Brothers and he has a charming smile. Or at least he did have one, before the advent of El Creepo.

Back to wonderful me. The best thing about my mother's infatuation with El Creepo was that her interest in *him* took the spotlight off *me*. You see, from the day I was born my mother has been ob-sessed with turning me into some kind of movie star, or celebrity, or jet-setter, or fashion model. She has spent my entire adolescence fussing over my hair and my clothes and my makeup. Dragging me to department stores. Taking me to beauty parlors. From the moment I hit puberty she began to model me like a lump of clay—but a lump I remained. And why? Because if nothing else, I was determined to march into adulthood as ME—a short klutzy person who was neither a beauty nor an intellectual, whose clothes came from thrift shops, but who did have a certain amount of character. If you will pardon the word.

So there I was that June—liberated from my mother's fixation on me, and also liberated from school—and trying to recover from a one-sided romance I had had with a boy named Jeffrey. One-sided is putting it mildly, because Jeffrey was gay, but I had been in love with him and was having a hard time getting over it. Jeffrey was a kid from Chicago, a dancer who had come to New York to break into show business, and I had fallen for him so hard that every part of me was still bruised. He had encouraged me to dress like myself, and keep my black curly hair very short, and he had told me that there wasn't anything I wanted in life that I couldn't have, and he had understood—completely—my passion for dogs. All I really care about in this world is dogs, and it was becoming clearer and clearer to me that whatever I did with my life was going to involve them. I would either be a trainer, or a handler, or a groomer, or a vet's assistant. With a rescue squad on the side, rescuing all of New York City's strays. The point is that Jeffrey had understood this. He had understood everything.

We had known each other for five months, and

then Jeffrey split. He had gone to L.A. to break into television—Broadway being too tough—and that was the end of it. Not even a letter or a postcard. Not even a phone call. So where my heart had been was now a very small wound—and where my happiness had been was a void. Jeffrey Collins, from Chicago, had moved on in life, whereas I was moving towards nothing. All I knew was that I did not intend to go to college in a year—no matter what anyone said— and that I did not have a friend in the world. I was turning into the biggest loner in my school, The Spencer School on 86th Street, and what was scary was that I did not give a damn.

People say they are loners, when what they really mean is that they are lonely. But not me. I was a *true* loner, in the sense that I belonged to no groups and participated in nothing. It is always possible to get into a group at Spencer because there are so many. The hoods, the jocks, the brains, the arty types, the addicts, etc. But I couldn't connect with any of them—so that weekends would find me sitting alone in the movies, or walking my dog, Happy, by the East River. I watched a lot of television. I slept too much. But the idea of connecting with someone just for the sake of connecting—like Shirley with Dr. Eisenberg—turned me to stone. What I wanted that summer was someone to talk to.

And then the letters began.

I noticed the first one instantly, though it was

tucked in with my mother's mail on the hall table, because the handwriting was so flowery. Just my name and address on the front, no return address on the back, and inside . . . well, what was inside was a shock. Because in the same flowery handwriting was a letter that said, "Dear Heidi Rosenbloom, You are everything to me. The light of dawn and the gentle purple of dusk. The stars glittering softly in the heavens, and the deep rotation of the earth as it turns. You are spring and sadness, lilacs and rain. Heidi Rosenbloom, my dearest, I love you."

No signature! And the handwriting was so delicate that you wondered if it could really be a man's. At first I thought it was a joke—and yet who was there to play a joke on me? I had no friends, and Jeffrey had moved away. Not that he would ever do such a thing—so who was there on the face of the earth who would want to write me such a letter? A complete put-on, of course, but who could have done it?

That night I lay in bed and tried to think of every single male person I knew—but none of them panned out. Would Jake, the elevator man, want to write me such a letter? No. My father? Don't be silly. Christopher Lee, the stand-up comic of the junior class? No. It was simply a dumb joke, and yet it bothered me that I couldn't figure out who the author was.

Two days later, another letter arrived. The same beige stationery. The same flowery handwriting.

"Dear Heidi Rosenbloom," it said, "I fall asleep each night thinking of you, and in my mind I hold you in my arms. You are early roses touched with dew, crystal lakes where swans gather. You are all the lonely beaches of the world, and you are also one bright sail in the sunset. Heidi Rosenbloom, my dearest, I love you."

I walked over to the full-length mirror in my bedroom and took a look at myself—a short plump person with a crew cut, a person dressed in boys' chinos and a boy's cotton vest. A person who, though Jewish, still wore Jeffrey's little gold cross around her neck. How could *anyone* think of me as a sail in the sunset? As a crystal lake? It had to be some kind of pervert. It might even be . . . someone who wanted to attack me.

No, I said to myself, that's just your New York mentality speaking. Your knowledge that you could be mugged in this city at any time of the day or night—mugged, raped, or kidnapped. Those are the thoughts of a New Yorker, Heidi, whereas this person is simply some kind of crazy romantic. Someone who reads poetry.

The trouble was that the more I stared at it, the more familiar the handwriting looked. It was true. I had seen this handwriting before, was familiar with it in some daily kind of way. God! I said to myself. This is upsetting.

When the third letter arrived, on June 10th, I be-

came alarmed. Because it said, "Dear Heidi Rosenbloom, These letters are only a prelude to my ap-
pearing in person. But I do want you to know that
I love you tenderly. You are the first snowfall in a
trembling forest. You are a white bird, taking wing
over the sea. Heidi, my dearest, I shall come to you
sooner than you know. Au revoir."

2

I was sitting at the dining table, finishing my morning coffee, while my mother read various items aloud from *The Investigator*—a scandal sheet she buys at the grocery store. She has always assumed that I find these tidbits as fascinating as she does.

"Listen to this!" she said, rattling the newspaper. "It says here that Jacqueline Susann once had an affair with Ethel Merman. Can you believe such a thing? It doesn't even make sense."

Since I could not remember who Jacqueline Susann was, much less Ethel Merman, I simply nodded and kept drinking my coffee. My mind was on those love letters.

My mother was in her morning costume of satin robe, pearls, and hair rollers. I, on the other hand, was in my usual costume of boys' pants, cotton shirt, and vest. We made an odd couple at the breakfast table each morning, but I will say this much for Shirley—she had stopped mentioning my clothes. After years and years of arguments—of me shopping at thrift stores and her dragging me to Saks Fifth Avenue—we had arrived at a stalemate. She would allow me to dress the way I liked as long as I did not use our building's elevator, thus shocking the neighbors. It was not exactly pleasant to walk down—and up—fifteen flights of stairs three times a day, but I figured it was good for my waistline. And Happy, my dog, liked it too.

At this moment, Happy was rolling around the dining room floor chewing on one of my slippers. "They are puppies until they are two years old," the vet had said to me—and Happy was just two. Since he had moved in with us he had eaten his way through a variety of shoes, leather belts and handbags, and Shirley was not overly pleased. Happy is part Cairn and part Norfolk, a small taffy-colored dog that I found running loose in Central Park. Without him I would probably be in an institution. In other words, he loves me and keeps me sane.

"Who was she married to, I wonder?" mused my mother.

"Who?" I said.

"Jacqueline Susann!" said Shirley, exasperated. "Was it Mike Todd? Marlon Brando?"

Well, even *I* knew that Marlon Brando had not

13

been married to someone named Jacqueline Susann, but I didn't have the heart to say so. One of the most frustrating things about my mother is that she always gets the facts wrong. To her, Freud was some German man who was addicted to cocaine, and T. S. Eliot was the person who wrote a musical called *Cats*. Now she had married Marlon Brando to Jacqueline Susann. However. It is better not to argue with Shirley when the subject is movie stars, because she has a very personal relationship with them. "Elizabeth Taylor lost the weight!" she would announce to me. "Alan Alda is on location again. His wife didn't go."

"Yes, I think it was Brando," she decided. "Though why a beauty like Jackie Susann would ever want a slob like him, I don't know."

I tried to keep my mind on the solution to those love letters. They came every two days now, and they were driving me nuts.

"The doctor and I are eating Polynesian tonight," said my mother. "It's a new place, near the Plaza."

It was only the beginning of the day, but I felt myself growing irritable. Because I could not stand the way my mother kept calling Manny Eisenberg "the doctor." It probably harked back to her youth in Larchmont, where a girl's biggest ambitions were to marry a dentist or a doctor and have live-in help. "The doctor and I are eating Japanese tonight," she would tell her friend Bobo Lewis over the phone. "The doctor is a real gourmet."

Three times a week El Creepo would take my mother to an exotic restaurant—and there, he would order the best of everything. He had a knowledge of wine too, said my mother, and made eating out an adventure. I thought of my father down in his Village apartment, living on Stouffer's frozen dinners and éclairs from the local bakery. I thought of his breakfasts of bagels and canned pineapple juice.

"I'll wear the navy silk again," said my mother. "The one with the long sleeves. The doctor likes it."

"Good," I said, trying to concentrate on those love letters and their dubious origin. But my mind was sliding back to the evening in May when I had first met Manny Eisenberg. The doctor. The podiatrist whose business card said, "Emmanuel Eisenberg, Complete Care For The Foot." Shirley had gone out with him for two weeks before she decided to have him meet me—the sixteen-year-old daughter whom the doctor could not believe she possessed. "He says I look too young to have a teenage daughter!" Shirley said gaily. "He says I look like a girl."

For some reason, Shirley had not been quite ready that night—her hair wasn't sprayed, her makeup wasn't right—and so she had left the doctor and me alone in the living room to get acquainted. "I won't be five minutes!" she called. "You two get to know each other."

I stared at Dr. Eisenberg, who was a very tiny, bald man—in his sixties, perhaps—and shuddered. He was carefully dressed, and very polite, but he was rather like a child. He was also the kind of Jewish person whose eyes fill with tears all the time. I mean, the doctor could not announce that it was Friday without being emotionally moved, and it was sort of tiring. Anything he mentioned about himself moved him to tears—his son Howard, his late wife Ethel, his relatives in Chicago.

"I lost my wife, you know," he said to me, his eyes filling up. "Two years ago, and I'm not over it yet. The condolence cards, you would not believe. I have a drawer full of them. She was a saint, my Ethel, a person who never thought of herself. And to the end of her life she allowed me to buy her nothing. Only a mink jacket, and then she never wore it."

How does one reply to a person like this? A person whose verbal style is strictly monologue? Does one say, "Indeed?" or, "How interesting." Or does one just keep one's mouth shut?

The doctor had moved on to the topic of his son, Howard. And the minute he said the word "Howard," his eyes filled up again. "The best private schools," he said to me, "the best universities. A Ph.D. in art history—which I approved of, which I find very interesting—and then what does he become? A nutritionist! Somebody involved with vitamins, with health-food stores. An expert on van Gogh, a *genius* on Monet, and he chooses to meddle around with nutrition. Vitamin C, he tells me, cures cancer! Vitamin B6, you should take for arthritis! Last week he tells me that AIDS—AIDS, mind you—can be slowed down by the use of alfalfa. A fortune spent on his education and he's talking to me about alfalfa."

"Indeed," I said—that being my word of choice at the moment.

"Ah, what can you do?" the doctor said in disgust. "They're all like that, the young people today. No reality. But his mother spoiled him. To her, he could do no wrong. She was too good, that woman, she let him walk all over her. Then, *then* when he's only eighteen she tells me that I should buy him a car. A car! I never had a car of my own till I was thirty, but she wants me to buy him a Honda. And that's when the trouble began, let me tell you, because he used that car like a weapon."

"Indeed, indeed," I said.

"Where do they go, the young people, when they drive around in cars? Do they know? Does anybody?"

"Actually . . ."

"Look," said the doctor, his eyes filling with tears again, "you seem like an intelligent girl. Your mother tells me you are very intelligent. So I ask you—do you think it is normal for a young man with a Ph.D. in art history to go into nutrition? To become involved with alfalfa?"

"Well . . ."

"I have been a doctor for more than thirty years. I worked my way through medical school and the residency almost killed me. My mother, God bless her, spoke not a word of English, but she encouraged me all the way. Thirty years I have been a physician! And not once have I seen a vitamin cure a disease. Oh, I don't say that it isn't fashionable to believe such nonsense. The most famous people in the world are writing books saying that they were dragged out of the jaws of death by the use of vitamins. But for thirty years I have been a physician and not *once* have I seen a vitamin cure a disease! And so what does he do—this privileged boy, this boy who went to the best schools in America—he becomes a nutritionist."

My mother emerged from her bedroom—her hair sprayed, her makeup perfect, wearing her best navy dress and three strands of pearls.

"My dear!" said the doctor, rising to his feet. "How lovely you look."

To my amazement, he kissed Shirley's hand. "Your charming daughter has been telling me all about herself," he said.

Which was perfect proof of El Creepo's sanity. He was a person who hogged every conversation, but at the end of the evening he always felt he had listened to *you.* "Tell me about your schoolwork," he would say to me, immediately launching into a diatribe against his brother Lou, who lived in Chicago. "Tell me about your grades," he would implore, veering into an attack on drugs, youth, and vitamin C. On and on. To the point where I would breathe a sigh of relief the minute he and Shirley were out the door. Off they would go—to yet another restaurant, to yet another new dining experience—leaving me and my dog in peace. How my mother could STAND El Creepo, I did not know—but he was male, and he took her out, and that, I guess, was enough.

"You are as dear to me as a young foal gamboling in a meadow," the last love letter had said. "You are as precious as the first pale jonquils of spring." And of course, no signature. The handwriting was so familiar! It was driving me nuts—and yet there was no one I could talk to about it. Which is one of the disadvantages of being a loner. Because there were times when I would have given anything to talk to another human being, yes, even to bore the pants off them, like El Creepo did to me. My one and only female friend, Veronica Bangs, had moved to California over a year ago. Jeffrey—as brief and elusive as a bird—was gone too. I talked to Happy a lot, but he was a dog, and never answered back. Maybe Shirley's liaison with El Creepo was not as crazy as it seemed. Because one had to assume that occasionally he ran out of breath and let her speak.

"You are as innocent as a kitten," the love letters said, "as fragile as dandelions. Wait for me, beloved, and be patient. Soon, I come."

3

"So what do they do together?" my father was asking. "Where do they go?"

"To restaurants, mostly," I replied. "To Broadway musicals."

"He has children?"

"Uh, yes, one. A boy named Howard who has a Ph.D. in art history. But he became a nutritionist."

We were sitting in Leonard's tiny, messy apartment on West 13th Street, and sun was pouring in the windows. It was a hot day for June, and Leonard was in his shirt sleeves, sitting at his rolltop desk. Instead of going out to a restaurant for lunch, we had shopped at the local deli and were consuming a meal of cold cuts, pickles, potato salad and sauerkraut. Happy was rolling around in a pile of Leonard's laundry, playing with a sock.

"I looked him up in the state medical directory," Leonard said. "The new one. He isn't there."

"Well . . ."

"Not that that means anything. But I hope your mother knows what she's getting into."

"In what way?"

"In *every* way," Leonard replied. "I just told you—the man isn't listed in the medical directory. I looked him up."

"I think he's genuine. I mean, his office is on Park Avenue and everything."

The minute I said "Park Avenue," I wanted to bite my tongue. Because the doctors Shirley goes to drive Leonard wild.

"Every doctor she goes to is on Park Avenue," he said. "Why should this one be any different? But he isn't listed in the directory, and I think that's a little strange."

I took a bite of my pickle. I had come down to Leonard's place to break some difficult news to him, but I still hadn't gotten around to it. What I wanted to tell him was that I had decided not to go to college—which meant that I didn't need the summer tutoring he had planned for me. In New York, the tutoring of prep-school kids is almost a cottage industry—but it was expensive all the same. "Daddy . . ." I began.

"I also called Bob Greenberg. You remember him from the old days, don't you? Bob the chiropractor?

And he said that a podiatrist would be listed in the directory. That is, if he's on the level."

"Daddy—I have something to tell you today."

"Hmmm?" said my father, looking around for his cigarettes. As usual, he had made a mess of everything, wax wrappers and cardboard cartons all over the place. Which is one of the things my mother hates about him. He is truly untidy. Shirley, on the other hand, is so neat that you cannot move a single object in our living room without giving her a nervous breakdown.

"Daddy," I said more firmly, "could we please stop talking about the doctor?"

Leonard looked surprised. "Why, of course baby. What's on your mind?"

Dogs, I wanted to say, my future in the world of dogs. My future as a groomer, or a handler, or a vet's assistant. If worse comes to worse, my future as a volunteer at the ASPCA. But instead, I said, "You saw how bad my marks were this year. I mean, a C average is pretty bad."

"Yes," he said patiently, "it is. But with a little tutoring, pussycat, you'll be up to par. I want you to have a good senior year at Spencer. And I want to go over those college applications with you."

Inwardly, I groaned. Because this was not going to be easy. My father, who never finished high school, has a very exaggerated opinion of higher education. I mean, he is a frustrated intellectual, a person who would have liked to have been involved with the better things in life, but who never got a chance because he had to work so hard. After slaving away in the Garment District in his teens, an uncle got him an apprenticeship to a jeweler on the West Side, and that began my father's career. Eventually he opened his own business and made a huge success, but he is a person who feels cheated.

"Did you bring those applications today?" he asked. "I want to study them before we start to fill them out."

"My guidance counselor is supposed to fill them out."

"So does that stop me from reading them? I want to see what's involved, that's all."

God, I prayed, please let me lose my fear of my father's temper. Let me just for today lose it completely. You remember how he once threw an entire Christmas tree out of the window of our apartment? And how it landed not two feet from an elderly woman who was walking her dog? God, if you remember all that, please help me today.

"Did you bring the one from Radcliffe?" asked Leonard. "That's the one I'm interested in. Harry Ferkser's kid went there and majored in physics."

"I'm not going to college," I said in a small voice. "That's why I came here today. To tell you that."

My father looked at me like I had just confessed to a murder. Like I had just told him that in a fit of rage, I had murdered El Creepo for the single purpose of shutting him up, of never again having to hear about his son Howard, or his brother Lou, or his saintly wife Ethel.

"*What* did you say?"

"I don't want to go to college, Daddy. I'm sorry to disappoint you, but I don't."

All the color seemed to drain from Leonard's face. "Have you said this to your mother?"

"No. Not yet."

"Then don't," he advised, "because it will only upset her. And you and I know that it isn't true. I've been planning for your college education from the day you were born."

He wasn't angry yet because he didn't believe me. He thought it was just some sort of a whim. As far as Leonard was concerned, the apex of my adolescence was going to be college—Radcliffe as a first choice, Vassar as a second.

He sighed. "Baby, you're just discouraged over those grades you got last year. But I've found a good tutor for you, one that your principal Mr. Kaufman recommended. His name is Mr. Darling and he's first-rate."

Mr. Darling, I thought. I don't believe it. "Daddy," I said, "I do not want to go to college. And if you make me go, I'll just run away or something. I hate school, *hate it*, and another four years of it would

24

give me a breakdown. I'm just not college material. I'm sorry."

And that, of course, is when he lost his mind. "What are you talking about!" he yelled. "What are you saying! If you aren't college material, then who is? You've had the best private-school education in New York, and in the summers you went to the most exclusive camps I could find. You are a well-mannered, brilliant girl, and I will not hear any more of this crap! What are you trying to do, give me a heart attack?"

God, I said silently, where are you? Hurry up.

"Please don't get so mad . . ."

"MAD? I'm not mad, I'm outraged. What do you intend to do without a college education? How do you intend to earn a living? Because I will not have you turning into a dependent person like your mother, someone who can't even balance a checkbook. You say she's dating some phony foot doctor? You bet your ass she is! Because the woman is so brainless she can't do one single thing alone."

"Daddy, please don't . . ."

"Brainless! Someone who just drifts around New York spending my money and buying junk. Jewelry, perfume, dozens of pairs of shoes that she never even wears. Don't you think I want a different future for you? And without an education there is no future."

"You never had an education . . ."

"You're goddam right!" he yelled. "And it wrecked my life! Do you think I wanted to be in the jewelry business, wanted to spend my days wheeling and dealing? I wanted something better, and when you're a little older you'll want something better too. I mean, my God, without an education what will you do?"

"I'd like to work with dogs. In some way."

As though he was a balloon that had been pricked by a pin, Leonard sank down in an easy chair. "Dogs?"

"Well, yes," I replied, knowing how awful the words sounded, how limp. "I mean, you know how much I love dogs, Daddy, how much I love Happy. So I'd like to work with them."

"You're talking like a child," he said wearily. "Like a little girl."

"I don't think I am. And anyway, it's *my* life we're talking about here. Not yours, and not Mother's. Why the hell should I go to college when I don't want to?"

"Don't swear at me," he said. "Don't make me any angrier than I am."

He rose to his feet, got a cigarette and lit it. Then he went over to the window and looked down on 13th Street. There was a traffic jam and horns were blaring.

I walked over to where Happy was rolling around

26

in Leonard's laundry, and picked him up. He licked my face and I buried my nose in his short, rough, doggy-smelling hair. "How's my sweetheart?" I said to him. "How's my love?"

I carried him over to a chair and sat down with him on my lap, feeling his little heart pumping. And suddenly I felt so depressed that I was frightened—and not because my father wanted me to go to Radcliffe. I was depressed because for years and years now my parents have talked about each other, to me, in a way that they should not. "A slob, a womanizer," my mother would say about Leonard. "A dumb bunny," he would say about her. "Did she ever open a book in her entire life? Does she even know where Europe is? Twice I took her there, and she wasn't sure which continent we were on."

Leonard turned and looked at me. And for a moment I wanted to take the whole thing back. I just wanted to apologize and tell him that of course I would go to college, any college he wanted. Because he looked terrible. "Heidi," he said, "I think you're going to change your mind about this—but until you do, I want to suggest something. I want to suggest that you take a job for the summer and see what working is like. You've never had a job in your life, whereas many kids your age work summers and holidays, just to have pin money. . . . Get yourself a job, baby, and try the whole thing out. Because as far as this summer goes, there will be no allowance."

Well, that one hit me hard. Because for as long as I could remember, Leonard had provided me with a very good allowance. I was used to having money in my pocket, was used to hopping in and out of cabs, and buying people presents. Now all that was about to change.

"See what it's like to work for your money," said my father. "And then, look into the future and try to decide which is better—working at menial jobs, like I did for years, or stepping into a place with a college degree in your hand. See what kind of *respect* people get who work at mundane things. Try the whole thing out."

4

Wanted, said *The New York Times*, airline secretaries and architects. Wanted, bakers and bookkeepers, computer operators, collection specialists. Wanted, nurses, physical therapists, pension administrators, real estate agents and restaurant managers. . . . I kept looking under "D," hoping to find something about dogs, but the "D's" were devoted to doormen and draftspersons, dentists, drivers and dietitians.

This is not going to be easy, I said to myself. This is harder than you thought.

I was sitting cross-legged on my bed while Happy lay on the floor, chewing a leather toy. My room—until recently a territory controlled and decorated by my mother—had undergone a change in the last month. Instead of a pink-and-blue boudoir out of the

18th century, adorned with velvet chairs and a glass dressing table, it was now a utilitarian place filled with Happy's toys, collars and leashes, and my ever-growing collection of dog books. I had bought an old print to put on the wall—one that showed some German Pointers, pointing—and was becoming more and more pleased with the whole effect. Shirley, on the other hand, said that it looked like the waiting room of a vet's office. But what the hell. This was my room. My refuge. My castle.

My mind veered away from the Want Ads to the letters I was receiving every two days. "You are the sun and the moon," the letters said to me. "You are spring and sadness, and fresh roses in the rain. Heidi, my dearest, sweetest little girl, I shall reveal myself to you soon."

But he didn't, and that was the most maddening part of the whole thing. He didn't reveal himself, he just kept on writing me those terrible letters about spring and sadness, roses and rain. About my hair resembling the midnight sky. About my eyes shining like secret sapphires. God! I thought suddenly, maybe it isn't a man at all. Maybe it's a woman. I mean, if Ethel Merman could have had an affair with Jackie Susann, then anything is possible. . . . Shirley, of course, had gone out and bought the biography of Susann in which these things were revealed, and she made a point of reading it aloud to me every day.

Wow, I thought, if it's a woman then I won't know what to do.

Who would call me a sweet little girl, a young foal gamboling in a meadow? Who would say, "Dear child, you are more lovely than you know." It had to be someone very old-fashioned. It might even be . . . Dr. Eisenberg.

"No!" I said aloud. And yet, was it so farfetched? The letters had started coming right after I had met the doctor, in late May. And the handwriting was flowery and perfect, like someone had learned it long ago. "Oh no," I said. "That one, I could not handle."

I began to pace my room, my hands clasped behind my back, searching for evidence that would reveal Dr. Eisenberg as a pedophile—a word I had recently learned in our sex education class. The doctor was certainly weird enough to be a pedophile, and there were times when his glittering eyes looked at me so strangely that I wanted to get out of the room. Maybe he had been to prison for such crimes and *that* was why he was no longer listed in the medical directory. For one second, I saw El Creepo doing hard time at Sing Sing, walking around a courtyard with the other prisoners, dressed in stripes.

Without knocking, my mother charged into the room, wearing her usual costume of satin robe and hair rollers. She looked around with distaste—as though she had entered a stable—and then she addressed the matter at hand. "I have just talked to your father," she announced, "just had a very long conversation with him, and what he told me, I find hard to believe. He told me that you do not want to go to college, that you are not filling out those applications."

I sank down on the bed. "It's true."

My mother opened her mouth and closed it again. It was evident that she was shocked. "What are you talking about? Everybody goes to college. Everybody."

"What about Ethel Merman?"

"I don't know what you're talking about, Heidi, but if this is some sort of joke, it's not a very good one."

"It isn't a joke. I'm not going. That's my decision."

Shirley looked around for a place to sit, and eventually chose a wooden chair I had found abandoned on 73rd Street. It was part of my new campaign to make my room mine.

"At least *paint* this chair or something," she said, sitting on it gingerly. "It looks filthy."

For a moment she seemed to forget the subject we were on as she gazed around the room. "I don't believe this place. It looks like your father's apartment downtown."

"Now, look Mom . . ."

"I know, I know, we made an agreement. But

could I bring anyone in here? No. Not even Bobo. It's a shame."

Bobo Lewis, who I have mentioned before, is a fat rich woman who lives in Westchester and whose house looks like a suburban version of the Taj Mahal. I mean, she is one of the most vulgar human beings on the face of the earth—so of course, she wouldn't like my room. My room would give her a stroke.

"And it smells in here, too," said my mother. "It smells of that dog."

"Mother, please . . ."

"All right, all right. But what you told your father shocked me very much. What will people think of us if we don't send you to college?"

"People? Which people?"

"What will they say, what will they think? They will think that we're ignoramuses."

"Who cares what they think? Whoever they are."

"Do you know how much money your father has spent on your education? Thousands. Even that nursery school you went to cost a fortune. And the summer camps! The best in America. You've had the best of everything."

"Why? I'm not a race horse."

Shirley chose to ignore that one. "So as far as we are concerned, this is just a whim, just some foolishness. I told your father the three of us would get together and discuss it."

I groaned aloud. Because the family meetings that

we had been having for the past three years always ended in disaster—with Leonard shouting and Shirley in tears.

"I'd rather not do that," I said.

For some reason, this made Shirley angry. "You will do what we say. You're not on your own yet, miss, just remember that. You're only sixteen."

"Sixteen and a half," I said quietly, but of course she didn't hear me. She was gazing around the room again, probably wondering what she could do to make it more attractive.

She put a hand up to one of her hair rollers that was coming loose. "The doctor and I are eating Bulgarian tonight. He's very much into Eastern European cooking at the moment."

"It sounds awful."

"Frankly," said my mother, "it *is* awful, but I would never tell him so."

"Why? What's so bad about the truth?"

"Heidi," said my mother patiently, "there are certain things you are going to have to learn about men. And the first one is—never tell them the truth. I mean, about anything. Because the truth is like Pandora's box, it just leads to trouble. Would I tell the doctor that I hate Bulgarian food? Of course not! Would I tell him that I have already gained so much weight, eating out, that I've enrolled at a fitness club? Would I tell him that sometimes—just occasionally—his breath is not too fresh? No, I would not.

Because a woman's job is to make her man comfortable at all times.''

Is he really "your man"? I wanted to say. Because if he is, he may also be a pedophile.

Instead, I said, "That sounds terrible to me. I mean, what's the point of having a man in the first place, if you have to deceive him?"

"Sweetie—when you're older you'll understand. At the moment, the only thing you care about is that dog.''

I looked at Happy, who had conked out on the rug, and who was snoring softly, and realized that it was true. I loved him better than anything on earth— my parents included—but what was wrong with that? Mom, I thought, your values are insane. You have concentrated your whole life on men, only to lose your husband and wind up with a tiny foot doctor.

"We don't agree about much, do we?" I said.

To my amazement, tears came into her eyes. Quickly, she brushed them away. "Don't be silly," she replied. "We're mother and daughter. Of course we agree.''

When she had left the room, I went back to my perusal of *The New York Times*. Wanted, it said, travel agents and traffic clerks, word processors and welders.

And then it hit me. Peter Applebaum, who was in my class at school, was going to Europe this summer with his parents. And Peter had recently become a professional dog walker. Someone would have to take over his dog-walking route for July and August—and that someone was going to be me. Wonderful me.

5

El Creepo was talking about his brother Lou, who lived in Chicago. No. "Talking" is not the right word. El Creepo was ranting and raving. Unfortunately, I was trapped in the living room with him while Shirley finished doing her makeup. They were eating East Indian tonight, down in SoHo.

"A mean man!" the doctor said to me. "An unfeeling man! Did he ever give his wife a piece of jewelry? Did he ever once take her to Florida? No, not a penny will he spend on anyone. He thinks that you take it with you, into the grave. Cash, jewelry, stocks and bonds—his safety deposit boxes are *crammed* with them, but did he ever once buy his wife a rose? A bouquet?"

"No," I replied. "Certainly not."

"And those boys of his!" the doctor said, his eyes

filling with tears. "They're just as bad, because they never had an example. To their mother they could do no wrong, but a father is supposed to provide an example. So what did they turn out to be? Bums! Loafers who smoke dope and play pool. Even as children, they would not clean their room or wipe a dish after supper. Help their mother with the dishes! Not on your life. They were out of the door before the meal was finished, out to God knows where, to play pool and smoke dope. To hang out! Yes, that's the word they use these days, hang out! My God, when I was their age I was holding down three jobs and going to medical school. I was a *ghost* in those days, a skeleton, and I would faint on the street from lack of food. But I was making a future for myself, and I knew it."

I edged away from the doctor, who was sitting beside me on the couch, so I could study him. He didn't seem to have a sexual attraction towards me, but you never knew. Maybe he was just a good actor. If I could get him to write something down, I could compare his handwriting with the love letters, but I didn't know how to do that.

"Your mother tells me you have a summer job," the doctor said. But before I could open my mouth to reply, he was off again. "Now I don't say that everybody has to be Einstein. I don't say they have to be Schweitzer. Such discipline is for geniuses only. But I *do* say that young people should at least help their mother with the dishes."

I glanced up and saw Shirley standing in the doorway of the living room. She looked weary and had on too much eye makeup. But when she saw that the doctor and I were aware of her, she brightened at once. "Here I am!" she said gaily. "Ready for the food of India!"

"My dear, my dear," said El Creepo. "You look stunning."

I watched as he held her jacket for her. "What are you going to do tonight, baby?" she asked. "Do you have a date or something?"

I sighed, because you could tell my mother a trillion times that people do not date anymore—that they go out in groups—and she still would not heed this fact. To her, youth means dating.

"Yes," I said. "I'm seeing Claude Debussy for dinner."

"Debussy?" said my mother. "What kind of a name is that? He's a foreigner?"

"Just a joke," I said lamely. "You two have a good time."

"I enjoy talking to you, Heidi!" said the doctor. "Your ideas are always very good!"

The minute they were gone, I took a small notebook from the pocket of my jeans, sat down, and began to study it. The notebook belonged to Peter

Applebaum, and contained all the information about his dog-walking route. He had, of course, let me have the route—only he had let me have it for a *fee*, which I had not expected. On the other hand, it was completely in character for Peter to do such a thing, because he is basically a crook.

I had phoned him two days earlier, only to learn that the person to whom he had loaned his route for the summer had changed his mind. "The route is available," he said over the phone, "but the fee is a hundred dollars."

"Fee? What fee?"

"Look, Heidi," he said in annoyance, "you don't think I'm going to give you my route for nothing, do you? You'll be earning eighty dollars a day with this job—and I think that's worth something."

"Eighty dollars a day? Wow. When should we discuss it?"

"Come over at three this afternoon. We'll work it out."

So at three o'clock I had turned up at Peter's apartment building on East End Avenue. A fancy building, where the doorman had to phone your name upstairs before you could board the elevator. A building that had a small waterfall in the lobby.

Peter met me at the door of his apartment in a rumpled shirt, pajama bottoms, and bare feet. He had a glass of liquor in one hand, a cigarette in the other, and looked forty years old. And how—I asked myself—*how* could I ever have found him attractive? Only three years earlier, when we had both been freshmen, I had thought he was the most beautiful boy in the world. Now, however, booze and cigarettes and pot were taking an early toll. Peter's dad is a Broadway playwright, his mother is a model, and his older sister is a jet-setter who does nothing but fly from place to place. Athens to Paris, London to Rome, Vienna to Frankfurt.

"Do you want a drink?" Peter asked.

"Uh, no," I said. "I don't drink much anymore. I don't like it."

"OK. Just wait till I refresh this one and then we'll have our conference."

He made himself a drink at the bar, and came over and sat with me near a window that looked out at the East River. His apartment, which I had never seen before, was really glamorous. Filled with paintings and mirrors and antiques—but I could see that none of it meant anything to him. He would have been just as happy living in a tunnel under Grand Central Station. "What are you going to do in Europe?" I asked, more out of politeness than real interest.

Peter shrugged. "Who knows? Get stoned, get laid. Something like that."

"Sounds great," I said brightly. "Where will you be? Italy?"

He gave me a bored look. "The French Alps. Look Heidi, let's get on with this thing, OK? I've got a lot to explain to you."

Which he proceeded to do. And he was right—because the routine was not exactly simple. Each day, twice a day, Peter walked eight dogs who lived between the 60's and the 80's on the East Side. All of the dogs were obedience trained, and all had their special place in the formation. The Dachshund, for example, was always second on Peter's right—while the Russian Wolfhound was kept third on the left. The English Bulldog was old and could not walk as fast as the others. He had to be accommodated. And the white Poodle was a prima donna and very difficult. The group of eight was walked in Central Park for exactly forty minutes, and then, in the opposite order in which I had picked them up, I would return them to their various doormen. "If it rains, of course, you take the dogs anyway," Peter explained. "Some of them wear raincoats."

"Do you like dogs?" I asked.

He took a sip of his drink. "Not particularly. It's just a job. My old man, you know, took away my allowance two years ago because I was in a bit of trouble."

"I remember," I said, Peter's trouble having been that he was caught dealing drugs. "Uh, do you pick up after the dogs? You know what I mean."

"Well," said Peter, "you're supposed to, but I don't. I mean, what the hell can they *do* to you if you don't? A little fine, that's all."

"I always clean up after my own dog. But eight dogs . . ."

"Right. It's a mess. Walk them someplace where there aren't too many people, and take your chances."

He handed me the notebook with the names and addresses of his clients, and I handed him one hundred dollars from my savings account. "So," he said, "that's that."

I looked at this disheveled kid, wondering again how I could ever have found him attractive, but also wondering if I dared ask his advice about the love letters. Peter was the most worldly person I knew, but something told me that my problems would not be of interest to him. For as long as I had known him, he had only been interested in drugs and sex. In that order.

"Well," I said, as he walked me into the hallway. "I certainly hope you have a good time in France."

"France, Italy, who cares? I only go because they won't leave me here by myself. I'd much rather be here."

Right, I thought, so you could hang out at Moby's on Third Avenue, where they accept those phony I.D.'s—and so you could make out with girls you meet at the bar. So you could get stoned and sleep in the Park.

"Have a good summer," I said.

He ran a hand through his hair and yawned. "Right. And don't screw up my dog route, OK? I'll need that route when I get back."

I walked home feeling very depressed. Because I would have liked to have confided in Peter about those letters. It was hard to be the kind of person I was, with no one to talk to and no one to help me if I ran aground. Not once in my life had I ever confided in my parents—so that whenever I would see, on television, the story of some kid who had committed suicide, and would hear his parents or neighbors saying, "Oh, but he was never like *that* at all. He was never depressed, always cheerful, always kind"—so when I would hear a story like that, I would have an immediate sense of recognition. Because who ever told their parents the truth? Very few people, that's who.

"You touch my heart like the saddest music, like the smallest flowers," a recent letter had said. "I look at you and tears fill my eyes at your youth and sweetness. These words must sound foolish to you, my dearest, but I mean them tenderly. Soon—so soon—shall we meet."

6

Two days later I was walking eight dogs in Central Park. Well, actually, with Happy it was nine, and my arms felt like they were going to break off. Peter's idea that these dogs were obedience trained was crazy. I mean, sometimes they were and sometimes they were not. And Happy, who was used to being walked alone, was furious.

So there I was, with a Dachshund, a Cocker Spaniel, an English Bulldog, and a white Poodle on my right—and a Scottie, a Russian Wolfhound, a Boxer, a Dalmatian and Happy on my left. There I was, with my arms aching, and my back aching, and all nine dogs pulling me across the grass. Happy, who found all of this infuriating, was tugging at his leash as though he wanted to make a jail break. And the English Bulldog, who was obese, kept holding all of us up. No sooner would Happy surge forward than the Bulldog would pull us backward. No sooner would the tall elegant Wolfhound try to spring ahead than the Spaniel would decide to stop and pee. It was so difficult! I wondered how I had ever gotten into it. However. Eighty dollars a day meant five hundred and sixty a week—and that is not exactly small potatoes. What were most teenagers earning this summer? Not five hundred and sixty a week. Daddy, I thought, you were wrong about this. Times have changed.

Peter had written down the dogs' names for me, but I was having trouble remembering them. The Dachshund was called Mitzi, and the Wolfhound was named Boris. The Bulldog was Simon, the Poodle was Toots, and the Scottie was MacGregor. The rest, I hadn't memorized yet. *"Heel!"* I yelled at all of them. *"Heel*, goddamit!"

No one heeled. They just kept bounding forward, pulling back, stopping to pee, stopping to sniff, then bounding forward again. The Russian Wolfhound thought he was in Russia, coursing the plains. The English Bulldog, I guess, thought he should really be at home having tea. Only the Scottie, MacGregor, kept a steady and sober pace. As for Happy, he was so angry that he just kept on barking and barking.

"SIT!" I screamed, as I sank down on a park bench. And, by God—don't ask me how—all of the dogs sat down. It was amazing. Even Happy sat down. The nine of them looked at me, as though to say, "So? What's next?"

"I have to rest," I said to them. "I'm beat." And at these words, every one of them lay down and put his head on his paws. It was unreal. For a moment we made a tranquil group—me and nine reclining dogs—but soon they were restless again. Only Mac-Gregor, whose character I was beginning to appreciate, studied my face to get the lay of the land.

I was near the 79th Street entrance to the Park, sitting on a bench that faced a little hill. The view was peaceful until three teenage boys approached. They were hoods, of course, like most teenage boys— including the ones in my school—but I was not prepared for what they said to me as they passed. It was very stupid, but it hurt my feelings to the point where tears sprang to my eyes. I will not repeat their dumb and filthy language, but it was all about my looks. My boy's clothes and my crew cut.

God! I thought. Are there no sensitive males in this world? Is every male either a degenerate like Peter Applebaum, or a bore like El Creepo? Have they no other interests but money and power and sex? Why don't I ever meet the nice ones, the ones who read poetry and send you flowers?

All of which brought Jeffrey back as suddenly as if he was sitting beside me on the bench. I saw his gentle face and bright blue eyes. His smile that was as sweet as a little kid's. I heard his wonderful

47

laugh, and I saw him dancing—dancing up a storm. Jeffrey had grown up in an orphanage, with not one single advantage, but he had turned into a beautiful human being. My friend in California, Veronica, had said that only I, Heidi, could have been stupid enough to fall in love with a gay boy. But I couldn't help it.

He hadn't loved me, of course, and he had made that very clear. But there was something about a kid who had been raised in an orphanage trying to break into show business that had touched me. Jeffrey was brave—which I was not—and had his whole life figured out. I, for the moment, only knew that I would be spending July and August struggling with eight pampered dogs.

By ten that morning I was back in bed, fully clothed, so tired that I could hardly move. Every part of my body ached from trying to control the Gang of Eight, as I thought of them—and the idea that I would be walking them again at four o'clock made me feel faint. No wonder this job paid eighty dollars a day. I am *worth* eighty dollars a day, I said to myself. At the end of the summer, I can give it all to a physical therapist.

My mother came into the room—and the sight of me under the covers fully dressed, startled her. She was wearing a pink jogging suit and had a pink sweatband around her hair. "What's this?" she exclaimed. "You're back in bed?"

"I'm just a little bushed," I said feebly. "It's my first day."

"Dog walking! With your education and background, you take a job as a dog walker."

"Right," I said.

"Bobo's niece is working in the court system this summer," Shirley said accusingly. "She's learning to be a court stenographer."

"Terrific."

"She's already met some very important people. But who are you going to meet in Central Park? Tell me that."

"Muggers," I said. "Rapists."

My mother let out an exasperated sigh. "Do you want a glass of juice or something?"

"No, no. I just need to rest, that's all."

"Well, all right. I'm off to the fitness club for a few hours."

The minute she left, I closed my eyes and let my mind drift. Jeffrey's face passed before me for a moment, and then I began to think about the grades I had gotten last term. I thought about my terrible grade in math, and my terrible grade in social science, and my terrible grade in English—which was a mystery to me, since I do like to read. But the trouble with my reading is that it does not lean towards fiction and poetry. It leans towards books on animals and arctic exploration.

"NO!" I said aloud, sitting straight up in bed. Because at last I had realized whose handwriting was on those love letters. "Oh, no!" I said. In my mind's eye, as clear as a photograph, was that same flowery handwriting on one of my English tests. In May, Mr. Moss, our English teacher, had given us a surprise quiz on modern literature. My own quiz had come back to me with this comment: *Heidi dear, the author of* Ulysses *was not Virginia Woolf. Will you kindly speak to me after class?*

Lionel Moss! My English teacher! The most handsome—and boring—person who had ever taught at Spencer. "Mossy Banks," as the kids called him, who was in his twenties and was trying to write a Master's thesis for Columbia University—on Rupert Brooke. He was a stultifying, crashing bore—but he was gorgeous to look at. "Oh, no!" I said again.

I hurried over to my closet, where I kept the love letters in a shoe box, and pulled one of them out. Then I hurried over to my desk and pulled out that surprise quiz. "Name the author of *For Whom the Bell Tolls*," the quiz had demanded. And I had said, Katherine Anne Porter. "Name the author of *Ulysses*," *the quiz had implored. And I had replied, Virginia Woolf. . . . Yes, the handwriting samples matched. The love letters were written in the hand of Lionel Moss.*

I sat down on the bed, stunned. And not only stunned, but frightened. Suppose Mossy Banks was crazy? Only a crazy person would try to approach one of his students romantically. You could get fired for doing such a thing. A parent could take you to court.

Calm down, I said to myself, those letters are about as threatening as a poem by Wordsworth. And Mossy Banks himself is so shy that he practically stutters when he speaks. He is shy and withdrawn, and has only been at Spencer for a year—teaching us English during the day and writing his thesis at night. He is not exactly Casanova. He is not Hugh Hefner. He is simply a very shy man who is devoted to Rupert Brooke.

I must pause here to tell you that Spencer has always had a very odd faculty. Our teachers were either graduate students, or failed opera singers, or defrocked ministers, or—like Frau Schneider who taught us German—elegant European people down on their luck. All owing to the fact that Spencer paid such miserable salaries. However. Since most of us kids were basically spies where the faculty was concerned, I knew a lot about Mossy Banks. Not only that he studied at Columbia, but that he lived on East 94th Street, that his favorite sport was walking, and that he frequented health-food stores. Once, only once, had he dated a teacher from the school—Miss Margolis—and she had let me know, in the most subtle way of course, that it had been the most boring evening of her life. He had taken her to the New-York Historical Society, to see an exhibit of old books, and then they had gone to a vegetarian restaurant. . . . I should introduce him to El Creepo's son, I thought, Howard the nutritionist. They'd be perfect together.

I was no longer tired, and my body no longer felt like a truck had run over it. Because I was determined to find out why Mossy Banks had been writing me those letters. It was inconceivable that he should be in love with me, but hell, anything was possible. Could I ever be in love with *him*? No way. He was as handsome as Robert Redford, but dull, dull, dull.

"You are the bright wing of a bird, seen fleetingly," his last letter had said. "You are heaped clouds, tinged with the sunset."

7

At ten the next morning, I stood across the street from Mr. Moss's apartment building. It was a nice building—brick, with a green canopy—but it wasn't exactly a hotbed of activity. Very few people came or went. I had already walked the Gang of Eight, delivered them back to their respective doormen, and now Happy and I were huddled in the entrance of a Chinese laundry—directly across the street from Lionel Moss.

Where are you? I said silently. Why don't you appear? But there was no sign of him. Maybe he had gone away for the summer or something. Maybe he had moved.

An hour passed, then two, and still there was no sign of Lionel Moss. Happy was restless and miserable, I was pretty restless myself, so I decided to decamp. It was silly to wait for him on the street when all I had to do was phone him. Yes, I would look up his phone number that very evening and demand an explanation. "Why have you been writing me love letters?" I would ask. "What is your problem?"

Would I be brave enough to say such things to a teacher? Why not? If he was brave enough to approach one of his students romantically, then I was brave enough to challenge him.

At four that afternoon I walked the Gang of Eight, plus Happy, around the Sheep Meadow in Central Park. The dogs were growing more accustomed to me and were not pulling quite as much—and I was beginning to understand their personalities. The Poodle and the Spaniel were spoiled brats who had never been taught a single thing—whereas the Wolfhound and the Boxer were willing to obey if you spoke to them firmly. The best of the group, however, was MacGregor, the Scottie. He would trot along at a measured pace, glancing up at me every few minutes to be sure things were OK—and then, when I told him that they were, he would return to his steady little trot. He had no sense of humor, but he was dependable, and that was what I liked about him. Happy liked him too.

My mother and the doctor were eating Cantonese that night—and as soon as they left the apartment, I pulled the hall phone into my bedroom and sat down at my desk. Lionel Moss's number was 555-2594—but as I started to dial, I hesitated. It was going to take a lot of chutzpah to tell Mr. Moss off, and I wondered if I could do it. He was, after all, my English teacher.

I put down the phone and went over all the things I was going to say to Mossy Banks. Words of criticism and outrage—but all coolly said, of course. The point was, to put an end to those embarrassing letters.

Taking a deep breath, I dialed 555-2594 and felt myself shudder as someone picked up the phone. "Hello?" said a familiar voice. "Moss speaking."

A wave of panic swept over me, but then I steadied myself. "Mr. Moss," I said, "this is Heidi Rosenbloom. I'm in your English class."

Which, of course, was a stupid thing to say—since he was all too aware that I was in his class. But we have two English teachers, the other being Miss Blampin, and I just wanted to make myself clear.

There was a pause on the other end of the phone, a long, terrible pause. And then the familiar voice said, "Heidi? Heidi Rosenbloom?"

"None other. I'm in your English class."

"I know that," he said softly.

And then there was another pause.

"Are you surprised that I phoned you?" I said, unable to think of anything else to say.

"Yes. I am."

"Well, I'm phoning you. Here I am, on the phone."

"Yes," he said.

It was evident that we weren't getting anywhere, and yet I was having trouble jumping into the water. I mean, what was I supposed to say to him, something like, "Are you psychotic, Mr. Moss? And if so, are you in treatment for it?"

"What can I do for you, Heidi?" he said after a moment. "Why did you call?"

I took another deep breath and said, "Because you have been writing me letters, Mr. Moss. That's why."

"Ah. So you figured it out."

"Yes, Mr. Moss, I did. I compared your handwriting to the handwriting on that test you gave us in May."

"Test? Ah yes, the little quiz. You said that Virginia Woolf had written *Ulysses*."

I felt a flare of anger, because I don't take criticism too well—probably because I have had too much of it all my life. "It was a perfectly reasonable mistake, Mr. Moss. I mean, Peter Applebaum once told you, in an essay he wrote, that Willa Cather had written *The Naked and the Dead*."

"I remember," said Lionel Moss. "In fact, the longer I teach the more I come to believe that no one reads anymore. Fiction, I mean."

"Well, you're right in a way. Kids don't read because there are always other things to do. We all have so many activities. And then at night, there's television."

"Yes," he sighed. "Television."

"To be perfectly frank with you, Mr. Moss, I don't like fiction. I mean, it's so . . . fictional."

"Go on."

"It's just that I don't know what fiction—and poetry—have to do with real life. The stories you see on the TV news are much more interesting than anything you could read in a novel. And also, more bizarre."

"Bizarre?"

"Of course. Like the other night, on the six-o'clock news, there was a story about a dwarf who had climbed Mount Everest. A *dwarf*, Mr. Moss, a person with every strike against him, climbed to the top of the mountain. I think that's fantastic. And just this morning, on the early news on NBC, there was a story about a cat who was left behind by its owners, when they moved, but who followed them anyway—all the way across the country. Three thousand miles! Which says something about the nature of cats, don't you think?"

"I do," said Mr. Moss.

"So many of the books on cats and dogs are simplistic. I mean, all they really tell you is that little cats

57

are just big cats who shrank, and that dogs are really wolves.''

''Do you have a dog?''

''I not only have a dog, Mr. Moss, I am walking eight dogs in Central Park twice a day. My father cut off my allowance this summer. I had to go to work.''

''Good heavens.''

''It's OK, really, because I'm earning a lot of money. It's hard work—walking eight dogs—but you get a lot of fresh air.''

''I walk in the park myself. Every morning.''

''You do? Gee. Maybe we could meet there sometime and have a cigarette together.'' Which was a stupid thing to say, since I do not smoke.

All of a sudden, I realized why I had phoned Mr. Moss in the first place. I felt myself blushing. ''Mr. Moss, what I really phoned you about was those letters. They've upset me very much.''

''I . . . I'm sorry to hear that,'' said Mossy Banks. ''I wouldn't upset you for the world.''

''Well, you *have* upset me. And I think we should talk about it.''

There was another pause, and then he said, ''Ah, very well. Why don't we meet in the Park tomorrow. We'll talk.''

''OK. That would be fine. We'll just . . . straighten the whole thing out. I'm usually at the Seventy-ninth Street entrance, off Fifth Avenue, at eight o'clock.''

58

"I'll meet you there tomorrow morning."

"Fine," I said. "Excellent. Good-bye now."

"Good night," said Lionel Moss, in that quiet voice of his. "Good night."

8

At six the next morning, I pulled myself out of bed and headed for the shower. I hadn't had enough sleep, but what the hell. My routine demanded that I shower and have breakfast between six and seven, pick up the dogs between seven and eight, and hit the Park at eight o'clock sharp.

I shampooed my short black curly hair, marveling at how easy a crew cut is to maintain—and then I chose a clean pair of jeans and a pale-blue shirt. My mother was still asleep, having been out late the night before, and so I consumed a cup of coffee and a blueberry muffin, and then Happy and I set off to pick up the Gang of Eight.

It was a typical July morning—with humidity hanging over the city like a blanket—but the streets weren't crowded and there was a nice smell in the air, like rain that hadn't fallen yet. I picked up my eight charges from their respective doormen—the Poodle, of course, was late coming down in the elevator—and then I headed for the 79th Street entrance to the Park.

Lionel Moss was waiting for me on the corner of 79th Street, and I must say he looked terrific. An expensive navy blue sweatsuit, and navy walking shoes, and a sweatband around his dark blond hair. Mr. Moss wears his hair long, but it never looks effeminate. And he has a good build, too, like an athlete. "Good morning," he said, gazing at a spot in the distance.

I felt myself tremble a little as I said, "Good morning."

Mr. Moss stared at the eight dogs—nine, counting Happy—and said, "I . . . I don't believe it. You walk all of them at once?"

"Sure," I said casually. "There's nothing to it."

We walked into the Park together—me, Mossy Banks, and the nine dogs—and headed west. I could tell that Mossy Banks was excited by this rendezvous because he couldn't look at me. And when our eyes did meet, by accident, he blushed.

As usual, the Dalmatian and the Spaniel were pulling my arms almost out of the sockets—while the Wolfhound and the Boxer made an effort to heel. MacGregor trotted along at his steady pace, looking neither to the left nor the right. It was as though the morning walk was a ritual he had to endure.

"What are their names?" asked Mr. Moss, as we headed for a grassy knoll.

I laughed. "You really want to know? OK, here goes. The Dachshund is Mitzi, the Wolfhound is Boris, the Bulldog is Simon and the Poodle is Toots. The Scottie is MacGregor, the Boxer is Clarence, the Spaniel is Alice and the Dalmatian is Spot. . . . Spot is a dumb name for a Dalmatian, and I don't like Alice much either, but there you have it. My own dog is named Happy. He's the one that's part Cairn."

"Amazing," said Lionel Moss.

As we continued to walk, I realized that we were about as close to having a personal conversation as we were to getting married. In the first place, Mr. Moss seemed incapable of eye-to-eye contact. He just couldn't look at me directly. And in the second place, he kept maintaining the conversation on a casual level. He talked about the dogs, the hot weather, and the Park, but he refused to get any more personal than that. He walked at a fantastic rate, and I had trouble keeping up with him. He was wearing a pedometer on his wrist.

"How long have you been walking?" I asked him.

"About a year," he replied. "Walking is *the* sport now. I love it."

"No kidding," I said, trying to keep up with him. He certainly walked fast.

"I have a book on walking that says that jogging kills, calisthenics cripple, diets debilitate and aerobics disable. And you know something? It's true. Walking is the only exercise that's safe."

"But people have been walking for centuries."

"True. But they have not been walking consciously."

We were approaching a bench, so I said, "Do you mind if we sit down for a moment?"

"Of course not," said Mr. Moss, averting his eyes. "Forgive me. I've been tiring you."

"Sit!" I said to the nine dogs, and they all sat down.

Mr. Moss seemed impressed. "That's wonderful. Do they always do that?"

"Yes," I lied, collapsing on the bench. "Wow, I'm bushed."

Since I wasn't sure what to say next, I asked, "Where do you get your gear, Mr. Moss? For walking, I mean."

He sat down beside me and gazed into the distance. "Over on the West Side. There's a place on Ninety-second Street called The Urban Walker."

"What do they sell there?"

"They sell walking systems. Everything you need to walk."

Wow, I said to myself, he's crazier than I thought. This is not going to be easy.

"I'll take you there one day," he said.

I looked at the nine dogs and saw that all of them were dozing. All but MacGregor, that is. He was staring down the path watchfully, as though protecting our group.

"It's wonderful to be with you today," Mr. Moss said quietly.

"Uh, yes," I replied.

He stared at a squirrel that was jumping from tree to tree. "I . . . I never dreamed that such a thing might happen."

"What thing?"

"Your phoning me."

He was giving me the opening I wanted, so I said, "Mr. Moss? I wonder if we might discuss those letters you sent me."

For the first time that morning, Mossy Banks looked at me. His eyes were the eyes of a dog lying by the bed of a sick master—the eyes of a dying deer, shot in the forest. "Did the letters offend you?"

"No, they didn't, Mr. Moss. Of course not. But they startled me. I mean, you're my English teacher."

"No longer," he said. "I quit my job last week."

"What?"

"I realized that I could not teach at Spencer and also love you. I felt that such a situation would be awkward for us both—and so I quit."

"God. How awful. But what will you do?"

"I've applied for a job at The Morrow School. Up in Riverdale."

"Morrow? Isn't that all boys?"

"Yes. I . . . I thought it might be a solution."

A solution to what? I wanted to ask, but I didn't have the courage. I mean, I was not just startled that he loved me—I was stunned. Because I must impress upon you once again that I am merely a short plump teenager with a crew cut. Greta Garbo, I am not.

Feeling myself grow bolder, I said, "Mr. Moss, are you really in love with me?"

He gazed at an airplane passing overhead. "Yes. I am."

"But I'm only sixteen and a half. And you must be at least twenty-five."

"I am twenty-three. But you know something, Heidi? In a hundred years we will be the same age."

"Isn't that a quote from someplace?"

"Yes. Bernard Shaw."

"I can't believe that you're in love with me, Mr. Moss. It seems so . . . weird."

"I have loved you from the day you entered my English class, a year ago. And the moment I knew I loved you was the moment when you said, in an open discussion, that you hated Elizabeth Barrett Browning's poetry, but liked her personally because she had a dog."

"But Mr. Moss, I'm not right for you at all. It's not

just the age difference, it's . . . everything. You're such an intellectual, Mr. Moss. You know things about literature that nobody else seems to know. When you talk in class, I can hardly believe it."

Which wasn't exactly the truth. Because Mossy Banks's English classes were so dull that most people slept through them. It wasn't that he wasn't smart. It was just that his mind was so erudite, so dry.

"Maybe that's the reason," he said.

"Huh?"

"Maybe I love you because you are so different from anyone I've ever known. So fresh, and young, and appealing."

I swallowed hard. "Mr. Moss, I don't think any of this is a good idea. I think it would just get us into trouble. Legal trouble, I mean."

He looked startled. "What?"

"I'm a minor. I'm underage."

"But my dear girl, I wasn't thinking of an affair! Is *that* what you thought? No wonder you were upset."

I do not believe this, I said to myself. Here we are, in the 1980's, and he is telling me that making out is not what he had in mind. So what did he have in mind? A series of seminars?

"But you quit your job," I said.

"Yes. I did. Because I did not want the situation to become awkward for us."

"Us," I thought. He's talking about "us."

The dogs were growing restless, so I looked Mr. Moss straight in the eye and said, "I have to get these dogs back to their homes—but before I do, I need to know one thing. Why did you write me those letters if you didn't want to make out with me? What was the point?"

He sighed, a sigh so deep that it seemed to come from the depths of his being. "We have a lot to talk about," he said.

9

It was two days later and I was sitting in a taxi with MacGregor, speeding down to East 23rd Street. MacGregor's owner, Mrs. Brown, had asked me to take him to the vet, and because I liked MacGregor I had agreed. Mrs. Brown, however, who I had never met before—because she left my paycheck with the doorman—was a surprise because she was not like her dog at all. She was a slovenly lady in her forties who had come down to the lobby of the building in an old bathrobe, and who had a cigarette hanging out of her mouth. She handed me the vet's address, a blank check, money for cabs, and then she split—making me realize that the old saying that owners resemble their dogs is completely fallacious.

As I realized that this was the first time MacGregor and I had been alone together, I cast him a sideways glance. He was sitting in the cab beside me in stoic silence, his eyes staring straight ahead. "It's only a checkup," I said to him. "Don't worry."

But MacGregor was not worried at all. One could see him trotting through the front lines of a war, secret messages hidden in his collar. One could see him in the Alps, coming to the aid of fallen skiers with little kegs of brandy around his neck. He had no sense of humor, but his character was impeccable, and I liked that. "It's only a checkup," I repeated.

I leaned back against the leather seat and thought about Lionel Moss. The idea that he was in love with me was so fantastic that I was having trouble absorbing it. In my entire life, no one had been in love with me, or even been attracted to me, so that the whole thing was going to demand some readjustment. It would have been much easier if Mr. Moss had been nuts, but he seemed to be perfectly sane. A little eccentric, but sane. We were going to meet that very evening at The Urban Walker, where he bought his stuff, and then he was taking me to dinner.

When you have spent sixteen years of your life thinking that you are weird and unattractive, too short, too plump, with eyes that are too small and a nose that is too big, with a voice like Woody Allen's and no evident charm . . . when you have spent years thinking of yourself this way, it is very hard to change the image. I tried to see in me what Lionel Moss saw—but I couldn't. All I saw was someone who bought her clothes at thrift shops and wore a crew cut.

Mr. Moss was terribly handsome—but how far could I go on his looks? Would looks alone help me to become attracted to him? Would his looks make up for the fact that his main interest in life was Rupert Brooke, a poet who had died in 1915? He was so obscure as a teacher—always mentioning the names of authors that nobody had ever heard of, always coming up with anecdotes about the Bloomsbury Group, or Henry James's sister, Alice. He did not just discuss 19th century literature or 20th century literature—he discussed *all* literature. One minute he would be talking about Thomas Hardy, and the next minute he would drift back to Dante's *Inferno.* Opinions of Katherine Mansfield would get mixed up with comments on John Updike. Mr. Moss loved authors so much that he made no differentiation between them. He loved Herman Melville and Truman Capote equally. He gave equal attention to Emily Dickinson and Irwin Shaw.

His teaching style was shy and reserved—like the rest of him—but once, last year in class, he had become very excited over Gustave Flaubert, who had written *Madame Bovary.* Acting out a little scene for us, Mr. Moss pretended that someone had asked Flaubert who Madame Bovary "really" was. "Madame Bovary?" cried Mr. Moss, pretending to be Flaubert. "Madame Bovary, *c'est moi!*"

That event had actually happened, Mr. Moss explained. It was a famous event in the history of literature. And the fact that Flaubert was not in our curriculum, did not bother him at all. What we were supposed to be learning was English Composition—so we could stagger into college—but Mr. Moss had forgotten that. He did not seem to know that he was teaching at Spencer. He thought it was Harvard.

The cab pulled up in front of MacGregor's vet, on 23rd Street. I paid the driver, and then I helped MacGregor down to the pavement. "There is nothing to worry about," I said to him. "I'm with you."

We entered the waiting room and I sat down, keeping MacGregor close by my side. The only other patients were two cats in carrying cases and a very old Collie. MacGregor glanced neither to the left nor the right, but simply sat there waiting his turn.

After a while, a young woman led us into an examining room. "Dr. Quinn will be with you in a minute," she said.

I glanced around, appreciating the fact that Dr. Quinn's equipment was very modern. Then he stepped into the room—a kind-looking man with gray hair. "It's MacGregor Brown," I said to him. "His owner asked me to bring him in for a checkup."

"Poor old MacGregor," said the vet, lifting MacGregor onto the examining table.

The comment startled me. "Is MacGregor old?"

"No, no," said the vet. "That's not what I meant."

Dr. Quinn gave MacGregor a full examination, clipped his toenails, and gave him some booster shots—an event to which MacGregor showed no reaction at all. "He's stoical, isn't he?" I said.

"He is indeed," said the vet, running his hand over MacGregor's coat. "You know, this coat could use some grooming. You might tell Mrs. Brown."

"I will," I said. "Thank you very much."

When I had paid MacGregor's bill and hailed another cab, I relaxed against the seat and took MacGregor onto my lap. "It wasn't so bad, was it?" I said to him. "Just a checkup."

MacGregor stared out of the window in steely silence. I wondered if he had been playful as a puppy, if he had ever had any fun. I wondered if he had grown up with other dogs. No, I said to myself, he didn't. He doesn't relate to dogs.

But he doesn't relate to people, either, I thought, as the cab pulled up in front of his apartment building. He doesn't relate to anyone.

After I paid the driver, I decided to take MacGregor up to his apartment myself. I usually left him with the doorman, but I was curious to see where he lived. So I stepped into the elevator and glided up to the tenth floor. Unlike most dogs, MacGregor showed no happiness at returning home. No barks, no tail wagging, no nothing.

After a long pause, Mrs. Brown answered the doorbell. She was still wearing her ratty bathrobe, and once again a cigarette was hanging out of her mouth. She gave me a bored look. "So?" she said.

I handed her MacGregor's leash. "He's fine. And he had his booster shots and everything. But the vet thought that his coat needed a little work. A little grooming."

"So what else is new?" said Mrs. Brown, unfastening MacGregor's leash from his collar. Joyless, he trotted into the living room and lay down.

I glanced around the living room. It was very messy—just like Mrs. Brown. "Have you had MacGregor long?" I asked, trying to sound pleasant and social.

"A year," she said. "My brother dumped him on me when he moved to California."

"Ah. I see."

"I would have had him put to sleep, but the vet wouldn't do it. He said he was too young."

Quelling the rage that was building up inside me, I said, "Really? How interesting. How old is he, do you think?"

"Who knows. Two, three. I don't know."

It was clear that she wanted me to leave, so I said, "Well, he's a very nice dog and I enjoy walking him every day."

"Right," she said, and then she closed the door.

I walked home feeling murderous. What a bitch the woman was! And what a tragedy that MacGregor should have to live with someone like that. No wonder he was silent and stoical. No wonder he showed no joie de vivre. Any other dog in such a situation would have had a nervous breakdown. But MacGregor hadn't because of his Celtic temperament. He was determined to endure.

The minute I got home, I picked up Happy and gave him a fierce hug. And as he wriggled with joy, I said, "Do you know how lucky you are? I mean, do you *know*?"

Still holding him in my arms, I went into my bedroom to decide what I was going to wear that night—for my date with Lionel Moss. Depositing Happy on the bed, I opened my closet door to have a look. Pants, shirts, and cotton vests. Coats and jackets from my favorite thrift shop, Grandma's Attic. Some boys' caps with visors. An Australian bush hat I had sent away for, for ten dollars. Hmm, I thought, this is not going to be easy.

At that moment my mother came in, looking exhausted. She was very dressed up—a linen suit, pearls, high heels—but she looked weary. "I've just come back from Sotheby's," she said. "The doctor and I stood in line for two hours to see the jewels— but we saw them."

The jewels she was referring to were the jewels the Duke of Windsor had once given to the Duchess of Windsor. They were on display at a place called Sotheby's before being auctioned off in Europe. I had about as much interest in them as I had in lumps of coal, but I tried to look alert. "No kidding," I said.

Removing Happy from the bed, my mother sat down and took off her high heels. "I wish you had come with us, Heidi. It was a spectacle. She had jewels the size of *fruit.*"

"No kidding," I said again.

"There was a whole collection of jeweled cats, and a nineteen-carat emerald engagement ring. There was a flamingo pin at least four inches long. Four inches of flamingo!"

I sat down at my desk and fiddled with an old doorknob I use as a paperweight. In an hour I would have to walk the Group of Eight, and then I would be meeting Mr. Moss.

"I don't know what he saw in her," Shirley continued. "I mean, she wasn't even pretty. But smart, yes, that I will give her. Smart as a whip."

"Right."

"It must have been a physical thing. And for that he gave up a crown."

You donated all your dresses to the Salvation Army, I said to myself, so you'll just have to wear jeans. Jeans and a shirt and maybe the plaid cotton vest. Why worry about it? Clothes are not the issue here.

"Bobo told me over the phone that people used to *pay them* to show up at dinner parties," said my mother. "Can you believe it?"

"Yeah," I said. "I believe it."

My mother unclasped her pearls, took off her jacket, and leaned back on my bed. She closed her eyes. "The doctor and I are eating American tonight, for a change. I don't know what to wear. He's seen everything I own." Upon which, she dozed off.

Which is one of the things about Shirley that has always amazed me. She can go to sleep at the drop of a hat, whereas I have suffered from insomnia from the time I was twelve. I gazed at her, realizing that she was beginning to look old. Well, not old exactly, but definitely middle-aged. Maybe I am adopted, I thought. Maybe she couldn't have any of her own, and she and Leonard went off to an adoption agency. . . . Because what other explanation was there? She was interested in the Duchess of Windsor's jewels, and I was interested in dogs. She shopped at Saks Fifth Avenue, while I bought my stuff at Grandma's Attic. And *she* would have gone out with Dracula, as long as he made a good escort, while I was about to rid myself of a tall blond man who most people would have found gorgeous.

To hell with it, I thought. I'll just wear my jeans and the blue cotton vest. To hell with the whole goddam thing.

10

Lionel Moss was waiting for me in front of The Urban Walker, and he looked wonderful. Dark slacks and a white shirt with a broad, open collar. Black shoes, highly polished. And his hair looked as though he had just washed it. It flowed down his neck in a blond stream. "Hi," I said.

As usual, he could not look at me directly, so he gazed about a foot over my head. "Good evening, Heidi."

He glanced at me for a split second, and glanced away. "Would you like to go into The Urban Walker and look around? It's very interesting."

"Sure," I replied. "Why not?"

The minute we entered the store, a little man wearing a hairpiece rushed up to us and shook Lionel's hand. It was obvious that he—Lionel, I mean—

was a steady customer. "Welcome!" said the little man to me. "Welcome to America's first walking store. Is there anything special I can help you with?"

"Not really," I said. "We're just looking around."

"Make yourself comfortable! I am Robert Balboa. I am here if you need me."

I walked around the store feeling amazed. I mean, the place was filled with hundreds of things for walking. There were walking outfits, walking shoes, walking poles, and walking socks. There were walking hats, walking gloves, and even walking underwear. All over the store there were signs that said, "Walk, Don't Die" and on a big screen a video was playing, showing you exactly how to walk. "Defying gravity, we lean forward to overcome inertia," said the voice on the video.

Lionel Moss came over to where I was watching the video. "Mr. Balboa is the city's foremost walker," he explained. "He has organized around fifty walking clubs."

"No kidding."

At that point, Mr. Balboa joined us. "May I help you charming people with something? May I be of assistance?"

"Uh, no," I replied, "but I find your store very interesting. The thing is . . . I just wonder why people need special clothes for walking."

Mr. Balboa smiled. "A good question—but one that is so easily answered! My dear, walking is not the same as jogging. Everyone knows that. And as far as the clothes go, they simply provide a little more style, a little more chic. I mean, where could you *go* in a jogging suit? Noplace. Whereas in a walking suit you could go into the Plaza and not be ashamed. Into Cartier's, even."

"Ah," I said, "I see." Which was a lie, because I didn't see at all.

Mr. Moss purchased a pair of summer walking socks, tucked them into his back pocket, and guided me out of the store. Mr. Balboa stood by the front window, watching us depart. He gave a little wave.

I stood on the sidewalk with Mr. Moss, who, of course, was staring directly over my head. "If you don't mind eating early, we could go over to the restaurant. I've made a reservation."

"Fine," I said.

I was afraid that he was going to take me to a vegetarian restaurant, as he had done with Miss Margolis, but not at all. He had made a reservation at a place called El Camino Real on Amsterdam Avenue. It was Spanish and had a lot of atmosphere.

The headwaiter led us to a small table and we sat down together. Mr. Moss shook out his napkin and placed it on his lap. He gazed at a potted palm behind me. "Would you like a drink first? A soft drink, I mean."

"Sure," I said. "Great." He ordered two Cokes with lemon.

Since it was clear that Mr. Moss was never going to look at me directly, I had plenty of opportunity to study him. How handsome he was! And his white shirt, with its broad lapels, was definitely romantic. On his left hand he wore a heavy gold signet ring. His fingers were tapering, yet strong.

Well, I said to myself, in a way it's too bad that you are going to get rid of him. Because he's very attractive, and he has good manners, and everyone would like him. Shirley would like him because he is handsome, and Leonard would like him because he is educated—and he could help you walk the dogs. It's too bad that the whole thing is inappropriate.

When the waiter brought our Cokes, Mr. Moss ordered us both paella—a dish with chicken and seafood and rice. Then he looked at me. It threw me a little. "Tell me about yourself," he said.

"Uh . . . what would you like to know?" I replied.

"Everything."

I had not intended to laugh at that moment, but it was a nervous laugh that came out. "Well, all right Mr. Moss, here goes. I am sixteen and a half and I don't have a friend in the world. I mean, not one. But I do love my dog Happy, and something tells me that that will be my profession. Dogs, I mean. But the whole thing is very difficult because my mother has always wanted me to be a glamor girl, while my father has always wanted me to be Albert Einstein.

They're divorced, by the way. My problem is that nobody has ever liked me the way I am, nobody but a boy named Jeffrey, and he moved to California. *Also*, Mr. Moss, to be perfectly frank with you, I hate school and have recently decided not to go to college. I suppose that shocks you—you in particular—but I've decided not to go. I want to work with dogs, that's all. Dogs."

I stopped myself. Because I was rattling on the same way I had the first night I phoned him. It wasn't appropriate.

"What an extraordinary picture you have of yourself," said Lionel Moss. "It . . . it stuns me."

"It does? How come?"

"Because you are so much more than that! *I* see you in a very different way."

"No kidding. Which way is that?"

Lionel Moss took a deep breath. "I see you as a free spirit—young, fresh, witty, and filled with hope. Oh, so many things! I think you are charming and funny, and bright and original. In short, I think you are wonderful."

Wow, I thought. He has *got* to be crazy. Bonkers.

"Mr. Moss, you've got it all wrong. I'm not like that at all."

"But you are," he said softly. "You are."

Our food arrived and we ate it in silence. And I was so shook up by the conversation that I didn't even know if the paella was any good. Mr. Moss had withdrawn into his shell again and was not looking at me. I ordered another Coke and tried to eat the food.

"Mr. Moss," I said, wanting to break the silence, "why don't you tell me something about Rupert Brooke?"

A look of surprise crossed his face. "Rupert Brooke? Would you be interested?"

"Yes," I said. "Yes, indeed."

Suddenly, Mr. Moss became animated—the way he did in class when something aroused him, something fascinating like Henry James's writing habits or Proust's asthma. "Very well," he said, "I'll try to tell you a little bit about Brooke's life. He was a handsome young Englishman who was born in 1887, and who was universally loved and admired. Had he not died in the First War, he might have gone on to become England's greatest poet. But fate struck him down, and he died of blood poisoning. His comrades buried him on the island of Skyros, off central Greece. The thing that was particularly sad about his death was that he had just fallen in love with a young actress in London. They had hoped to be married."

"Gee. That's terrible."

"It was indeed, because she was as beautiful as he was handsome—a girl named Cathleen who was to become world-famous years later. When he was away at war, he wrote her this:

"We have found safety with all things undying,
The winds, and morning, tears of men and
mirth,
The deep night, and birds singing, and clouds
flying,
And sleep, and freedom, and the autumnal
earth."

"That's beautiful," I said.

Mr. Moss gazed above my head. "They never became lovers, and when he died she cursed herself that she had never had a child by him. A child, at least, would have been a symbol of their love."

"Why didn't they become lovers?"

"Who knows? The morals of the time, her scruples, his honor. My God, who knows. What I am trying to learn right now was whether or not she ever visited his grave, on Skyros. She's dead, of course, and there is very little written about either of them. I may go to Greece next year and try to discover the truth."

"For your thesis?"

"Yes," he said softly. "For my thesis . . . and for him."

For a moment, there was nothing left to say. Mr. Moss looked a million miles away—and in my own mind Rupert Brooke and his young actress were running through fields of wildflowers, somewhere in England. I saw him sitting in a theater, watching her act. I saw her on the deck of a ship that was heading towards Greece. She would kneel at his grave and place flowers there.

Mr. Moss had ordered something called flan for dessert, which turned out to be a custard, and as I ate it I wondered how Lionel Moss had maintained himself, thus far, in the modern world. I mean, he was definitely a romantic in an era where "romance" seemed to be reserved for those terrible paperbacks you see in the drugstore. Here was everyone in America sleeping with everyone else—communicable diseases notwithstanding—and there was Mr. Moss involved with Rupert and Cathleen. Where did you *come* from? I said silently to Mr. Moss. Where did you grow up? A monastery, perhaps, in Tibet.

By the time we were sipping our coffee, I had decided that 1) Mr. Moss was a virgin 2) he was harmless 3) he was never going to make a pass at me. But then, as the check arrived and he paid it, he caught my eyes with his.

"Would you like to come over to my place?" he asked. "We could listen to music."

11

Lionel Moss's two-room apartment was as neat as a monk's cell. Very little furniture, and books from floor to ceiling. Rows and rows of books, alphabetically arranged, by poets and novelists, historians and biographers. The floors were bare and polished, the lighting was soft, and there was only one picture in the entire place—an oil portrait of a woman.

Mr. Moss put some classical music on the stereo, and offered me a glass of Evian spring water. I took it and sat down on a velour couch. His furnishings were definitely old-fashioned.

He sat across the room from me on a straight-backed chair, listening to the music. It was Ravel or something, very romantic, and as it continued he began to hum the melody. He looked more handsome than ever, but I did not feel comfortable with him. . . . I glanced at my watch and saw that it was still early. Had it been later, I could have made some excuse and split. Nope, I was stuck for a half hour at least.

Since the oil portrait was on the wall directly across from me, I studied it—a woman of forty or fifty, with short white hair, in a red hunting jacket. There was a riding crop in her hand. A Great Dane sat by her side.

It should have been a Beagle or a Foxhound, I thought. When you ride to hounds, you need a *hound*. "Uh, is that a relative of yours?" I asked Mr. Moss. "The lady in the picture?"

His face brightened. "It is indeed. My Aunt Clemence. I grew up with her."

Since this was the first piece of personal information Mr. Moss had given me, I pricked up my ears. "No kidding. Where was that, exactly?"

"In Virginia."

"Aha," I said.

"Her full name is Clemence Vale," said Mr. Moss, as though I should recognize it. I didn't.

There was a pause, and then he said, "Clemence Vale, the mystery writer."

"Oh," I said evasively, "yes, of course. How come you grew up with her?"

"My parents died in a car accident when I was five. Clemence raised me."

He walked over to the stereo and turned off the music. Suddenly, the silence in the room was profound. Then he turned and looked at a spot just to the right of my left ear. "I love you," he said.

Since I had not expected him to say that, I choked on my spring water. "Mr. Moss . . ."

He came and knelt by my side. "Please," he said, "*please* call me Lionel. Every time you say Mr. Moss, I feel like dying."

"OK," I said nervously. "I'll call you Lionel."

The fact that he was kneeling by my side made me very uneasy. "Mr. Moss, I mean, Lionel . . ."

He took my hand and kissed it. "You are so lovely."

I retrieved my hand and held on to it firmly with the other one. "Lionel . . ."

"You cannot know what it means to me to have you here, in my home. A dream come true."

I felt very confused. Because in one way, he was making out with me—and yet in another way, he wasn't. "Lionel," I said again, "this whole thing is making me nervous. Would you please get up?"

His face fell. "Am I disturbing you? Upsetting you? Or is it that you too feel the magic between us?"

Magic, I said to myself. If this is magic, give me death.

"Mr. Moss, I'm sorry, but I really do not want to make out with you. Please forgive me. I mean, that

87

was a very nice dinner and everything, but . . ."

He rose stiffly to his feet. "Is that what you think I am doing? Making out?"

"Well . . ."

"Heidi, I'm in *love* with you. Do you think that I would do anything to offend you? Do you think that I would compromise us both?"

"Tell me about your aunt," I said.

If I had wanted to distract him, that was the way to do it. "My aunt?" he repeated. He looked a little dazed.

"Yeah, your Aunt Clemence. The writer."

Mr. Moss returned to his chair on the other side of the room. "My aunt," he declared, "is a remarkable woman, a woman of genius. She is the author of thirty books, five of which have been made into films, and I am amazed that you seem not to be familiar with her work. Her last book was called *A Thousand Ways of Dying.*"

"Gee," I said, "I thought there was just one."

It was supposed to be a joke, but Mr. Moss didn't smile. "It's about a killer who freeze-dries his victims. My aunt's books are famous for their ingenious methods of killing. In the one she's writing now, the killer discovers that his victim is allergic to bee stings. So he ties him up, smears him with honey, releases five hornets, and that's that."

"How horrible."

"It is indeed. As a person, of course, Aunt Clemence is nonviolent. She wouldn't hurt a fly."

"What about her hunting?" I said suspiciously. "She had her portrait done in hunting clothes."

Mr. Moss smiled. "Oh, that. Just a little conceit of hers. The house in Virginia is filled with portraits of her, and all in different costumes. My favorite one is Auntie as the Blue Boy."

"It should have been a Beagle. Or a Foxhound."

"Beg pardon?"

"The dog in the picture," I explained. And then one of those silences fell over us.

You're lucky, I told myself, luckier than you know. Because in a few minutes you will leave here and no harm will have been done. You will just get out, and put Mr. Moss and his aunt behind you. He is not crazy, he is simply eccentric. And you can get rid of him easily. Just tell him that you have a steady boyfriend. Tell him you are engaged.

I rose to my feet. "Well, it's been very nice . . ."

Mr. Moss came over to me. "Don't go yet. Please don't. Let me look at you just a few moments longer."

"OK," I said.

He reached out a hand and touched my hair. "How beautiful you are, Heidi. How pure."

"Mr. Moss . . ."

"Lionel," he said gently.

"Lionel," I repeated.

In one more minute he will be kissing you, I told myself. Come on, Heidi, *split.*

But I didn't. I just stood there as he stroked my hair with his long tapering fingers. His face was flushed and his eyes looked very bright. "I have to go," I said feebly. "Really."

We walked to the door and stood there together. And for a moment I could not get over the fact that this handsome man was in love with me. When would such a thing happen again? Never. I would live out the rest of my life in the company of dogs.

He was gazing at me openly. No longer did he avert his eyes and no longer did he stare into the distance. He was gazing at me with a terrible kind of worshipful love. Like a Springer Spaniel. Like an Irish Setter. "You are wonderful," he said. "Utterly and completely wonderful."

12

The following morning I was walking around the Sheep Meadow in Central Park. I did not feel the nine dogs who were almost pulling my arms out of their sockets, nor did I feel the light rain that was falling. All I could think about was the note in my pocket addressed to Lionel Moss. I had composed it late the previous night, explaining that I could not see him again—explaining that I was engaged to a young man who was in Europe at the moment. In Prague. I thanked Mr. Moss for the Spanish dinner, and I thanked him for the Evian spring water and the Ravel. "I hope you find what you are looking for in life," my note had concluded. "Au revoir."

Because of the inclement weather, some of my charges were wearing raincoats. The Dachshund, for example, was wearing a little yellow slicker, while the English Bulldog had on a coat made by London Fog. The Poodle was wearing tiny galoshes—but MacGregor, of course, wore nothing. Far be it from Mrs. Brown to do *anything* for MacGregor but feed him and send him to the vet once a year.

"Buck up, MacGregor," I said to him. And he cast me a little glance over his shoulder. "It's OK," said the glance. "I am a Scot. I am used to bad weather."

A young man passed me, jogging, and gave me a quick smile. In the second that our eyes met, I saw that he was very cute. Not handsome, like Lionel, but cute. Twinkly eyes and a turned-up nose. "Hi," he said as he passed, and then he was gone. God! What I wouldn't have given for someone like that to be attracted to me—someone young and normal.

I did a quick inventory of my love life and came up with very little. Some fooling around, when I was ten, with a boy named Bobby Tyler. A crush, at age twelve, on the kid who used to deliver our groceries, Pablo Gonzalez. Then a crush on Peter Applebaum, based solely on his looks. Then Jeffrey—a true love, but an impossible one.

A meager record, for someone about to become a senior in prep school. A sad record, too. Because what it revealed was that no one found me attractive.

No one but Lionel Moss.

It was raining harder now, and I only had on jeans and a cotton Windbreaker, so I headed back towards Park Avenue to return the dogs. As briskly as possible, I delivered seven of them to their doormen, but kept MacGregor for last. I had a wire dog brush in my back pocket and wanted to give him some grooming.

As soon as I was in MacGregor's lobby, I tied Happy to the leg of a chair and started to brush MacGregor. He gave me the most startled look in the world, but did not protest. He probably hadn't been brushed for a long time.

I ran the wire brush through his shaggy coat. The doorman was giving me dirty looks, but I did not care. I just kept on brushing MacGregor's damp shaggy coat, trying to give it some luster, some form.

"There," I said to him at last. "There, old man. That's better."

MacGregor looked at me—and I swear I could see a flicker of gratitude in his eyes. I mean, I *know* that I am too anthropomorphic, that I give animals human characteristics, but I felt that MacGregor was grateful. Immensely pleased with myself, I sent him up in the elevator.

As I walked home in the rain with Happy, I kept thinking of all the things about Lionel that were an enigma. He had been raised in Virginia, but had no Southern accent. And he lived pretty well, for a teacher. Most of our teachers were poor. Had the gold signet ring belonged to his father? And why would his aunt want to dress up in costumes and have her portrait painted? I tried to imagine Lionel making love to someone, but could not get him into a bed. I tried to imagine him naked, but his clothes wouldn't come off. In my mind he was permanently dressed.

As I entered the lobby of my apartment building, the new doorman, Clarence, hurried up to me. "Miss Rosenbloom? I have some flowers for you. The boy just delivered them."

"Flowers? No way. There must be some mistake."

Clarence shook his head. "No, no, it's your name on the card. Look here."

He handed me a dozen red roses, wrapped in cellophane. Attached to them was a card with my name and address on it. "Wow," I said.

Clarence looked interested. "Aren't you going to read the card?"

I glared at him. "I'll read it upstairs."

Fortunately, my mother was not home—so I took the roses into the kitchen, filled up the sink, and placed the stems in water. Then I opened the card. "I love you," it said. "L. Moss."

I pride myself on being a fairly cool person, but those roses shook me. I mean, they were absolutely gorgeous, with long stems and buds that were still tightly closed. Their leaves were a glossy green. A faint odor emanated from them.

Getting out a pair of scissors, I cut the stems on an angle, as I had often seen Shirley do, and then I placed the roses in a vase of water. Happy was watching all this, wagging his tail, and I leaned down and patted him. "How many people get a dozen roses in the middle of the week?" I asked him. "Tell me that."

With Happy trailing behind, I took the roses into my bedroom and put them on my desk. The buds were beginning to open a little and the smell was intoxicating. "Lionel," I said, "you're too much."

It occurred to me that somewhere in my closet was an anthology of English and American poetry, a textbook we had used in the eighth grade. I rummaged around in the back of the closet, and by God, there it was. I looked Rupert Brooke up in the index. Pages 300–302.

I skimmed Brooke's poems until I found one that I remembered. It was called "The Soldier" and I had a faint memory of reading it long ago.

If I should die, think only this of me;
  That there's some corner of a foreign field
That is for ever England. There shall be
  In that rich earth a richer dust concealed;
A dust whom England bore, shaped, made aware,
  Gave, once, her flowers to love, her ways to
    roam,
A body of England's breathing English air,
  Washed by the rivers, blest by suns of home.

I closed the book and sat at my desk for a while—thinking of Rupert who had loved Cathleen, and thinking of Lionel who loved me. The poem wasn't bad once you adjusted yourself to it, once you realized that people really used to write that way. I mean, Keats and Shelley were flowery too, and yet their poetry was the poetry of the times.

It was then that I reached into the back pocket of my jeans and found the note I had written to Lionel the night before. The farewell note.

I had forgotten to mail it.

13

I was sitting in the dining room, having a cup of tea with Dr. Eisenberg, while my mother conducted a long phone conversation in the hall. Bobo Lewis had met a new man and wanted to talk about it. Meanwhile, the doctor and I sipped our tea. In a little while, he would be taking my mother to a van Gogh exhibit at the Metropolitan Museum. Unlike his son Howard, the nutritionist, El Creepo was very much into art. He had given Shirley a membership to the Met for her birthday, and now they went there every Wednesday. It was beginning to occur to me that maybe my father had been right about El Creepo's medical credentials. He had a lot of free time for a doctor.

"Young people!" the doctor was saying. "No morals, no nothing. Living together is what they call it, when it's merely a convenience. But I ask you, what protection does a young woman have in such a situation? None! When my brother told me that his son Donald was living with a girl I almost fainted. He isn't twenty yet! And the girl is eighteen. What does a young woman know at eighteen years of age, I ask you."

"Well . . ." I began.

"No morals and no standards," the doctor continued. "It's like musical chairs. In *my* day, believe me, we made a commitment. You wanted to sleep with a girl, you married her. That was it, kiddo, no fooling around, no musical chairs. And did it make people unhappy? No! It gave them stability. OK, so maybe the husbands fooled around a little, but it never interfered with the home life. The home life was sacred. Also, in the old days Jewish people did not divorce. It wasn't even considered. You married a woman, you stuck with her for life."

"Right," I said, sipping my tea. "Right," I said, reaching for a cookie.

We were sitting at the dining table together—the doctor rambling on about marriage and commitment, while I thought about Lionel Moss. I had not mailed that note to him. Instead, I had phoned to thank him for the roses and we had made another date. For tonight.

People come in twos, I told myself. Adam had Eve. Napoleon had Josephine. Ronald Reagan had

Nancy. . . . People come in twos, and my mother may be right. A woman needs a man—and Lionel, at least, is handsome and kind. Look at Leonard. He has no one in his life and he's miserable.

I was still seeing my father for lunch every Saturday, and when I had told him that I would be earning over four thousand dollars for the summer, he had almost fallen into his veal with lemon sauce. We were eating at Giorgio's that day, in the Village, and he had looked stunned.

"Four thousand?" he said. "What do you mean, four thousand?"

I took a sip of my Coke, trying to seem blasé. "Well, I'm earning five hundred and sixty a week. So for two months it will be four thousand, four hundred and eighty dollars."

"That's crazy," said my father. "What do you do for that kind of money?"

"I walk eight dogs. Twice a day."

He shook his head and ordered another martini. It was a very hot day and he looked pale and tired. He was wearing a natty summer suit with a pinstripe, but it was rumpled. "OK," he said, "so you'll be earning four thousand dollars for the summer. But baby, it has nothing to do with your future. For your future, you need an education."

"Why? Why can't I just go on walking dogs?"

"You talk like a child, Heidi. What do you see yourself doing at forty? Walking dogs?"

"Yes."

He sighed. And for a moment I felt sorry for him, because from his point of view he was right. It *would* be a bit eccentric to wind up as a middle-aged dog walker, but who ever said I was normal? At least I would be spending my life with animals. At least I would not be sitting in an office.

I looked around the restaurant and saw that it was filled with tourists, the kind of people who invade New York every summer. "We saw the Empire State Building yesterday!" a woman at the next table was telling her friends.

"You're forcing me into a corner," said Leonard. "You're forcing me to come down hard on you."

"How do you mean?"

He finished his meal and took out a cigarette. "Baby, you've had a pretty soft life. Freedom, pocket money, a trip to Mexico with your mother . . . you've had it all. But if you refuse to go to college, you'll have to make your own way in the world. No more dough from the old man."

But I'm already making my way, I thought. I'm earning eighty dollars a day—and I can continue to do so. To hell with Peter's dog-walking route. I'll get a route of my own.

"I can take care of myself," I said stiffly. "What makes you think I can't?"

"Kids," Leonard said sadly. "You give them everything, and then they tell you they never wanted it in the first place. They take your money and then accuse you of *having* money. It's crazy."

I came out of this reverie to see the doctor helping Shirley into her raincoat. It was pouring outside, and they were off to the museum. "We'll only be a few hours," Shirley said to me. "You're sure you don't want to come along?"

"No," I said. "Thanks anyway."

"Van Gogh," she said brightly. "A very unstable person. They say he tried to cut off his nose."

"His ear," I said. "It was his ear."

When they had gone, I roamed around the apartment looking at things. I was rarely conscious of material things, but Leonard's edict that I would soon be out on my own worried me. One day Shirley would move to a smaller place—she might even marry El Creepo—and then where would I be? I strolled around, with Happy at my heels, looking at the paintings Leonard had bought one summer in Paris, looking at Shirley's antique love seat and brocade-covered chairs. A grand piano, Persian rugs, silver on the sideboard in the dining room, a real Tiffany lamp. Did any of it mean a thing to me? No, I told myself, it didn't.

That evening Lionel and I sat in a French restaurant on Eighth Avenue and 53rd Street. Somewhere in the same neighborhood my mother and El Creepo were dining too. Maybe these evenings should be combined, I thought. Maybe we should double-date.

Lionel had ordered salmon for both of us, and as we waited for it to arrive we sipped our drinks. He was drinking white wine tonight, which surprised me. I was having some Perrier.

". . . loneliness," he was saying. "And it's not quite the same thing."

"Huh?" I said. "I'm sorry. My mind wandered."

Lionel smiled. "I was just saying, dearest, that solitude and loneliness are different things. I mean, I have been solitary most of my life, but never lonely."

"Good," I said.

As always, Lionel looked wonderful—dark gray slacks, and a cream-colored cotton shirt. He had on a tie, but it was loosely knotted, poetically knotted. His eyes looked piercing and bright. But how boring he was! A crashing bore.

Also, he was doing something that really bothered me, which was that he kept calling me dearest, and darling, and my love. When our dinner rolls arrived, he had said, "Will you pass me the butter, darling?" and when the waiter spilled my Perrier, he had declared, "Never mind, love. We'll get you another."

". . . for ages," he was saying, "and yet no one knew it. I couldn't tell Aunt Clemence, and there was no one else to tell. So I retreated into books. That's always been the way with me—books and more books."

"Right," I said, having no idea what he was discussing.

"I was often sick as a child, and so of course I read a lot. Auntie's library is huge, over ten thousand volumes. She really should have her own librarian."

He smiled, as though this was a witty remark—so I smiled too. "Do people do that? Have their own librarians, I mean."

"Of course, darling. But one has to be rich to do it."

Are you rich? I wanted to ask him. And are you a virgin? The first item doesn't matter to me, but the second one does. "Tell me more about your life," I said.

Lionel gazed at me. There were candles on the table and they cast a flickering light on his face. A strand of blond hair fell over his eyes. He brushed it away. "All right, dearest. But I'm afraid it will seem dull to you. I lived with my parents in Baltimore until I was five. Then, when they were killed in the accident, Auntie took me in. I was awed by her, almost afraid of her. She seemed so . . . perfect. You'll be meeting her one day. You'll see what I mean."

I'll be meeting her, I thought. Why?

"She sent me to military school when I was eight, and I had a rather dreadful time there. I was too delicate, too shy to get on with the other boys. And that was when I decided to improve my physique, to become good at sports. . . . After military school, I went to the University of Virginia, and then, a year ago, I came to New York—to work on my Master's thesis. Auntie and I, you see, had had a disagreement. I decided to strike out on my own."

"What kind of disagreement?"

Lionel blushed. "It's rather a long story."

I'll bet it is, I thought. Oh Lionel, why are you so dull? You have the face of a movie star and the soul of a dusty old scholar. It's a shame.

"Did your aunt ever marry?" I asked Lionel.

A strange expression came over his face. "Ah, no. She didn't. For many years she lived with another woman. Cornelia."

Another woman? I said to myself. Aha. Like Ethel Merman and Jackie Susann. "Cornelia?" I said politely.

"Cornelia Wesley-Burke. The novelist. A platonic relationship, of course."

"Of course," I said. "Of course."

At that moment, the waiter brought our food—salmon with a cream sauce, and potatoes and fresh beans. It looked very good.

We ate in silence, and then Lionel ordered strawberries for dessert. I sat there wondering when we were going to get down to the nitty gritty. In other words, the subject of him and me.

As we ate our strawberries, a musician began to stroll among the tables, playing on a violin. That sounds corny, but it wasn't. It was beautiful. He was playing a Brahms sonata, Lionel explained. I turned and watched him.

When I turned back to look at Lionel, he had taken my left hand. And not only had he taken it, but he was putting a ring on it. "This was my mother's," he said, "and now it's yours. Your engagement ring."

"What?" I said. Several people turned and stared.

"Shhh," said Lionel, putting his hand to my lips. "Shhh, my dearest."

I looked at the ring he had placed on my left hand. It was a blue stone, surrounded by little diamonds. "It's very precious," Lionel said gently. "Just like you."

"Lionel, my God . . ."

"Shhh," he said again. "Let's listen to the music."

14

I am engaged, I said to myself, as I lay in bed that night. I am engaged to be married. . . . It was midnight and yet I could not fall asleep. I just kept feeling the ring that was on the fourth finger of my left hand, running my thumb over its smooth blue stone and little circle of diamonds. The stone, Lionel had explained, was a sapphire.

How had all this happened? One minute I had simply been Heidi Rosenbloom, dog walker—and the next minute I had become the fiancée of a man named Lionel Moss. "Heidi Moss," I said aloud, but the words didn't sound right at all. "Heidi Rosenbloom Moss," I said, and that didn't sound right either. Suppose my mother found out! She had already been so curious about the roses that I'd had to tell her I had bought them for myself—which she didn't believe for a minute.

Calm down, I told myself. You don't have to be engaged unless you want to be. You can just give back the ring and say that the whole thing was a mistake. A misunderstanding.

I did not want to be engaged to Lionel Moss . . . and yet, was it such a bad idea? In one short year I would be on my own, and Lionel could help me. I don't mean that I wanted him to *support* me, but he could help me start a full-fledged dog-walking business. I would encourage him to finish his thesis. We could live in the Village and have lots of dogs and read poetry at night.

The only fly in the ointment was that I did not love him—but how much did that matter? I had loved Jeffrey, and he had left me. My mother had loved my father, and he had left her too. Did romantic love matter in a relationship? And who, besides Lionel, would ever find me attractive?

I groaned and pulled Happy closer to me. Against Shirley's wishes, he sometimes slept with me, his head on my pillow. "You are my real love," I said to him, and then I fell asleep.

What a terrible dream I had that night! I was in Central Park, and I was not just walking nine dogs, but ninety. In each hand I held forty-five leashes and the dogs were pulling me forward at a rapid pace.

They pulled me deeper into the Park until we arrived at the carousel, where Lionel was waiting for me with a minister. The wedding, the minister explained, would be on the carousel and the bridesmaids would be dogs. But then the ninety dogs jumped onto the revolving platform and turned into wood. . . . I woke up screaming.

My mother rushed into the room. "Heidi? What is it? What's the matter?"

I shook myself awake. Happy was looking at me as though I was crazy. And so was my mother. "A dream," I said. "A nightmare."

Shirley sat down on the edge of the bed and felt my forehead. "Do you have a temperature? Are you sick?"

"No . . . I just had a bad dream."

"You've slept through your alarm clock. It's seven-thirty."

"God!" I yelled, leaping out of bed. "I'll be late for the dogs."

I threw on my clothes, grabbed a quick cup of coffee, put Happy's leash on him and raced out of the apartment. It was the first time I had ever been late for the dogs and I felt awful. And, of course, every one of them was waiting for me—watched over by an irate doorman. "Look, I overslept," I said to the Spaniel's doorman. "I'm sorry."

"This lobby is not a kennel," he said coldly.

Go drown yourself, I thought, but bit my tongue.

Soon I had picked up all eight dogs and was heading for the Park. As the group of us sailed through the 79th Street entrance, that same kid I had seen before passed me. The jogger. The one with the turned-up nose. "Hi," he said as he passed, and gave me a little grin. "Hi," I said.

And then he was gone—a very cute boy who I would liked to have met. Who, perhaps, I would like to have loved. A cute, normal boy with twinkly eyes and brown hair. But instead of such an alliance, I was now engaged to Lionel. Lionel, who could talk to you for five hours about James Joyce's days in Zurich. Lionel, who had a crush on Virginia Woolf. Lionel, who could tell you all about Thomas Mann's exile from the Nazis.

However. A decision is a decision—and by eleven that morning I had decided to let the engagement stand. It would be a *long* engagement, I told myself, long enough for me to find out if I could bear to sleep with Lionel. How would the two of us ever get into bed? Lionel was so formal, so considerate. He would probably want to discuss the whole thing first. But if sex didn't work for us, what else was left? James Joyce wandering around Zurich. Virginia Woolf's friendship with Sackville-West. The real meaning of *The Magic Mountain* by Thomas Mann.

I stopped at a bookstore and bought three mystery novels by Clemence Vale. In paperback. "Pretty gory stuff," the saleslady said to me. "No kidding?"

I replied, perusing the titles. Along with *A Thousand Ways of Dying*, I had bought *Aquamarine* and *Death on Demand*.

Dragging Happy behind me, I headed for a bench near Hunter College, over on 68th Street and Lexington. It was a place where I often sat and read while college students milled around. I sat down in my favorite spot, told Happy to "sit," and began to skim the books.

Clemence Vale's plots were so gory that I could hardly bear to read them. In one book, a decapitated head is kept in a refrigerator. In another, a body is placed in a huge fish tank in a madman's private aquarium. The body sits there on the bottom as exotic fish swim by. "A million copies in paperback!" said the blurb on the back of *Aquamarine*. "America's foremost mystery writer!" said another blurb.

That night, after dinner, I read *Aquamarine* from cover to cover. I hated it—and the amount of explicit sex in it surprised me. Then, continuing with my homework, I opened my eighth-grade poetry textbook and began to memorize one of Rupert Brooke's poems. It would please Lionel if I knew some of them by heart.

They say that the Dead die not, but remain
  Near to the rich heirs of their grief and mirth.
  I think they ride the calm mid-heaven, as these,

110

In wise majestic melancholy train,
   And watch the moon, and the still-raging seas,
And men, coming and going on the earth.

" 'They say that the dead die not,' " I began aloud—but then there was a knock at my door. I went and opened it and found Shirley standing there. All of which was strange, since knocking is not in her repertoire.

"Can I come in, baby?"

"Sure," I said. "Be my guest."

She stepped into the room, shuddered at the way it looked, and went over to sit on my wooden chair, the one I had found on 73rd Street. To please her, I had painted it green. "It smells in here," she said. "It smells of dog."

I turned Lionel's ring around, so that the stone faced my palm. "Do you want something, Mom? I was reading."

She pulled her satin robe around her more tightly. It was obvious that she wanted to tell me something, but didn't know how to do it. Finally, she said, "I'm going away this weekend. The doctor is having a house party at his place on Long Island."

"Really? How come?"

"What do you mean, how come?" she said in annoyance. "How come what?"

"How come he's having a party?"

"That's a ridiculous question, Heidi. He's having

111

a house party because he wants to entertain some friends. I will act as hostess for him."

"Sounds great."

"There will be two other couples there," she said defensively. "And a housekeeper."

"Good," I said.

"I mean, the doctor has this house on Long Island and he never uses it. Manny, I said to him, you have a lovely house that you never use. And you're paying a housekeeper to live there. Open the place up, invite some friends!"

"Right."

"We'll go on Saturday morning and come back Sunday night. You'll hardly notice I'm away."

"Right."

"Don't just keep saying *right* to me, Heidi. You sound like a moron."

"What do you want me to say?"

"Oh, you're impossible," she said, rising to her feet. "You simply will not communicate."

Communicate, I thought, what am I supposed to communicate about? So you're having an affair with El Creepo. So what? It isn't my business.

But later, as I sat there thinking about it, I got very depressed. Because nobody likes to think of their parents having affairs. It is just too uncomfortable to contemplate such a thing, and the fact that El Creepo was little and bald made it worse. I mean, I don't think I would have felt so badly if she had been off for a weekend with Cary Grant. Had he been alive, I mean.

I heard Shirley running the tub in her large Hollywood-type bathroom, her bathroom that is filled with marble and glass and indirect lighting, and dozens of perfume bottles and cosmetic jars. And as I listened to the sound of the water, I decided to phone Lionel and invite him over for Saturday. If we were ever going to make love together, now was the time. And I didn't want to be a virgin any longer.

I would ask him to stay all night.

15

"Lionel," I said, "why don't you come over and sit with me on the couch? You're so far away."

Lionel blushed and took another sip of his demitasse. It was eight at night, we had finished the meal I had cooked for us, and now we were sitting in the living room. Wow, I said to myself, this is not going to be easy. He looks like he's at a funeral. How are you going to tell him that he's spending the night? That you bought him a pair of pajamas at Bloomingdale's?

Lionel sipped his coffee and gazed at the paintings on the wall. He gazed at the grand piano and Shirley's antique love seat. But he did not gaze at me.

"How's Mr. Balboa?" I asked. "Your friend at the walking store."

For a second, Lionel brightened. "He's fine, Heidi. As a matter of fact, I saw him only today."

"You did? No kidding."

"He's carrying a new line of walking underwear and I wanted to have a look at it."

I tried to imagine Lionel in walking underwear, and failed. "Have you been walking much lately?"

"Of course. I walk ten miles a day."

I wondered why anyone would want to walk ten miles a day, but did not say so. I glanced at the clock and saw that it was eight-thirty. What was my mother doing at this moment? Better not to think about it.

Lionel had arrived at six o'clock with a plant, an African violet, into which he had tucked a small bottle of perfume. Surrounding the whole thing was pink tissue and ribbon, so that it made a very pretty gift. I had been encouraged by this beginning . . . but then things had gone downhill. I mean, here we were, on opposite sides of the living room.

The silence was so profound that I could hear Shirley's bedside clock ticking. And since Lionel was gazing at the floor, I cast him a sidelong glance. He looked wonderful, as always, in expensive slacks and a poetic-looking white shirt. No tie. Polished brown shoes. He looked wonderful, but he also looked embalmed.

As the silence continued, I tried to think of what

I liked about Lionel—and came up with the fact that I liked him because he resembled MacGregor. Not physically, of course. But he had the same kind of humorless dependability, the same kind of courage. A person could count on Lionel, just as a person could count on MacGregor. They were very much alike.

There was a mirror on the wall across from where I was sitting, so I took a quick look at myself. Yep, I looked good—new jeans and an Indian shirt I had bought at the thrift shop. I had shampooed my hair that afternoon and it looked curly and soft. I had shaved my legs and put colorless nail polish on my nails. I had placed a dab of Shirley's Chanel No. 5 behind one ear.

"You know," I said casually, "I've been reading the poems of Rupert Brooke lately. They're pretty good."

Lionel seemed to wake up. "*Have* you, Heidi? How amazing."

"Not at all," I said. " 'They say that the dead die not, but remain near to the rich heirs of their grief and mirth.' "

"For heaven's sake! Have you been memorizing them?"

"Sure. Of course."

"Well, for heaven's sake," Lionel said again.

He took another sip of coffee and stared at the

floor. "Don't you want to come over here?" I asked. "You look so uncomfortable."

He was sitting on one of Shirley's brocade-covered chairs. They were 18th century, and very small. Lionel rose to his feet. He advanced across the room. He sat down next to me on the couch, and I breathed a sigh of relief. So far, so good.

"You look handsome tonight, Lionel," I said—and the minute the words were out, he turned the color of a tomato.

It was evident that he wanted to change the subject. "Ah, have you been doing your summer reading?" he asked. "Have you looked at your reading list?"

The list he was talking about was one that he had given us on the last day of school, in early June. He had handed out copies of it and everyone had groaned. Because on this list were twenty authors to read over the summer. People like Virginia Woolf and Flaubert. People like Chekhov.

"Actually," I said, "I haven't gotten around to it yet, though I did buy a copy of *Orlando*. By Virginia Woolf."

Lionel looked appeased. "Good, Heidi, good. You will love that book once you get into it. It's a sort of metaphysical romp."

I edged closer to him. He smelled of expensive soap and aftershave lotion. He smelled of cotton, freshly ironed, and he also smelled of Lifesavers. It was a heady combination. "You're so attractive," I said.

Lionel blushed scarlet. He cleared his throat. "Thank you."

Why aren't I more experienced? I asked myself. If I just had some experience, I could seduce him. But I don't know what I'm doing, and neither does he. He's a virgin, just the way I am. A virgin, in the last part of the twentieth century.

"Are you a virgin?" I said.

He jumped as though I had pinched him. *"What?"*

"Nothing, Lionel. Forget it."

I went across the room, chose a record of Shirley's, and put it on the stereo. Maybe music would help to soften him up. If not, then this whole evening was going to be a bust. The record I put on the machine was an old Judy Devero one. She was singing "Divine."

"Am I yours?" sang Judy Devero. "Are you mine? Is this thing that has happened between us really divine?"

I returned to the couch and sat down. "Lionel . . ."

He turned and looked at me with his gentle eyes. "Yes, Heidi?"

"Uh, Lionel, my mother is away for the weekend. She's in Northport, Long Island. For the weekend, that is. So if you would like to stay here tonight, that would be fine with me.''

All the color seemed to drain from his face. "What are you talking about?"

"This," I said. And then I kissed him.

Well, OK. It was our first kiss, so I didn't expect it to be overwhelming. But neither did I expect it to be quite as flat as it was. I had kissed Lionel with all the skill I possessed—the skill that my friend Veronica and I had developed together, when we were twelve and had practiced kissing by the hour—and yet it did not arouse him. My lips could have been a dead fish, pressing against him.

Not to be daunted, I kissed him a second time—but it wasn't much better. His lips were tightly closed. *Meanly* closed, in a way. It was awful.

"Do you care?" sang Judy Devero. "Can you sleep? Are there nights, my darling, when you too must weep?"

I brushed a lock of hair away from his forehead. "Lionel—don't I attract you at all?"

"Heidi . . ."

"My mother is away for the weekend, Lionel."

"Yes, I know."

"We could make love tonight, Lionel. If you wanted to."

"I know."

He rose to his feet and walked over to the window, where he stared out at the city. Meanwhile, Judy Devero continued to ask her lover those difficult questions.

Lionel turned to face me. He looked like he was about to give a speech—and that was what he proceeded to do.

"Heidi," he said, "at this very moment, here in this room, you are wearing my mother's ring—her sapphire ring that Dad gave her in the 1950's. Surely you must realize that I would never have given you that ring if I didn't love you, if I didn't, actually, worship you. But there are certain principles that a person must adhere to. Now I suppose it is very old-fashioned of me not to believe in premarital sex, but I don't. For twenty-three years I have been saving myself for the woman I love, and you, Heidi, are that woman. I must therefore insist that we wait until marriage before we consummate our passion. Anything less than that would shock and dismay me. I mean this seriously, Heidi. I do."

He finished the speech and stood there, waiting for me to respond. But all I could see was an image of Lionel and me on our wedding night, trying to consummate our passion. We were lying in bed completely clothed, and he was reading Virginia Woolf.

"OK, Lionel. If that's the way you want it. I mean, I would never force you to do anything. You know that."

A look of relief came over his face. "Thank you."

I walked him into the foyer, and we stood there gazing at each other. "Well . . ." I said.

He took my hand and kissed it. "I've had a lovely evening, my dearest. Thank you so much."

"You're welcome."

"Such a delicious dinner. Did you cook it from scratch?"

"Yes. I did."

He smiled. "You are so adorable, and so very young. Whenever I look at you, my heart falters."

"No kidding."

"Yes," said Lionel, in his element again, "my heart falters with happiness, and I hear the song of a nightingale. In *that* way, little Heidi, do I love you."

16

It was the middle of August and I had decided to kidnap MacGregor. No more taking him home every day to a mean, uncaring owner. No more lying awake at night, wondering if he was being fed. Yep, I was going to invent some kind of scenario for Mrs. Brown, and then I was bringing him back to my house. Shirley would have a fit, but I did not care. MacGregor was someone who deserved a new chance in life—and I was going to supply it.

What I had decided to tell Mrs. Brown was that MacGregor had pulled away from me in the park and run after another dog. I had chased him, but with so many dogs in tow I hadn't been able to catch up. The last I had seen of MacGregor was his little black tail, disappearing over a hill. It was too bad, a terrible shame. I would alert the cops and also place an ad in *The New York Times.* . . . As for Shirley, she was so involved with the doctor that she might not even protest a new dog in the house. She had come home from her weekend in Northport in a very strange mood—one that I had interpreted as depression mixed with resolve. In other words, I felt that she hadn't had a good time, but that she did not intend to admit it. She and the doctor still dined together three times a week, and spent Wednesday afternoons at the museum. "He's phasing out his practice because he has a slight heart condition," Shirley explained to me. "In a few months, he'll retire."

Which explained why El Creepo had not been listed in the new medical directory. He was phasing out his career. He would move to his house in Northport, and I was beginning to fear that my mother would go with him. Was it possible that Shirley would marry El Creepo and become a Long Island housewife? Cool it, I said to myself, you have Lionel.

Which was the point of the whole thing. Lionel loved me. Lionel brought me flowers. Lionel had even written me a poem that rhymed "nightingale" with "not for sale." "Unlike the Chinese nightingale," the poem said, "my fragile heart is not for sale."

And I could talk to him, too. About anything. About all the loneliness of the last years, and about not going to college, and about loving dogs. He didn't understand me completely, but he tried. He listened and nodded and tried to comprehend. Now that sex was out of the way—for the time being—we did a lot of things together. We visited The Urban Walker and chatted with Mr. Balboa. We went to restaurants, and we bought books, and we read Rupert Brooke aloud. The only thing I did not do with Lionel was bring him home to meet Shirley—because I knew that she would find him very odd. He would kiss her hand and launch into a discussion of Flaubert. He would bring her flowers and try to discuss James Joyce.

On the morning that I decided to kidnap MacGregor, I headed over to MacGregor's house with a kind of fierce determination. I would walk all the dogs, return them, keep MacGregor with me, and take him to my place. Then I would go over to confront Mrs. Brown with the news that MacGregor had run away. The whole thing was terribly dishonest, but I didn't know how else to do it.

However, that is not the way it worked out— making me realize that a bumper sticker I once saw on a Buick had the right idea. "Life," said the bumper sticker, "is what happens while you're making other plans."

To begin with, Mrs. Brown was waiting for me in her lobby, which was highly unusual. She was wearing her ratty bathrobe and she had MacGregor with her. It was evident that she wanted to talk to me. "Hi," I said. "Good morning."

"Do you have a minute?" she asked. "I want to tell you something."

Since MacGregor was always first on my list, I had not yet picked up the other dogs. I tied both him and Happy to a brass railing near the elevator, and turned to face Mrs. Brown. "What can I do for you?"

"Let's sit down," she said. And we went over and sat on a bench.

She puffed away on her cigarette for a moment. Then she gave a sigh and said, "Look, it's this way. I just can't keep him anymore."

"Keep who?"

"The dog," she explained. "He's too much of a burden. I mean, I can't even go away for the weekend, for God's sake. It's like having a child."

"Well, sure," I said, wondering where this conversation was going.

"I'm not like you, Heidi. You're an animal lover. Me, I'd rather have my freedom. No kids, no animals."

"Sure. I know."

"This person in Connecticut, a lawyer, invites me to come up for the weekend, and I can't even go unless I bring the dog. And this person doesn't like dogs."

"Right."

"So what am I left with? I'm left with a dog and no social life."

"I understand."

"This person has a tennis court and a heated pool, for God's sake. And I have to refuse his invitation because of a dog."

"Yes. I understand."

"So it makes me angry," she declared, "and what is worse, it makes me depressed. And depression is dangerous for me. My therapist has been saying that for years. So what I'm going to do is this—I'm going to give the dog to that shelter on Fifty-ninth Street. They do *not* put them to sleep there. They find them homes. And look, let's face it, the dog doesn't even like me."

Like you? I thought. You're lucky he hasn't murdered you.

"Why not give him to me?" I said, trying to sound casual. "I'd be glad to have him."

Mrs. Brown looked astonished. "You would?"

"Sure. MacGregor and I get along fine. And Happy likes him too."

Mrs. Brown blew a stream of smoke into the air. "Well, for God's sake. I never thought of that. You really want him?"

"Yes. I do."

"What about your mother?"

"My mother is crazy about dogs. She can't get enough of them."

"Well, OK. That's a very good solution. You want to take him this morning, or what?"

"I'll take him after the morning walk."

"Good, good. Just drop by here and I'll have his things ready for you."

"Right," I said.

I headed up Park Avenue with MacGregor and Happy, and my heart was pounding as though I had just been given a million bucks. Because I loved MacGregor and now he was mine. I would soon be the owner of two small dogs—one black and one taffy-colored. "MacGregor?" I said.

He gave me a glance over his shoulder and kept to his steady pace. We were on our way to pick up the Dachshund. "MacGregor," I said, "you're my dog now."

And then I stopped, right in the middle of Park Avenue, and knelt down and kissed him. MacGregor looked shocked. But Happy seemed happy about it. He barked a few times and wagged his tail.

All during the morning walk my heart was singing. Oh, I knew what was going to happen when Shirley found out, but I felt I could handle it. I gave the dogs a brisk walk for forty minutes, delivered them all back to their doormen, and then made my way down to Mrs. Brown's building. Happy and MacGregor, I noticed, were trotting along in tandem.

I rang Mrs. Brown's buzzer in the lobby, and she said over the intercom that she'd be right down.

Soon she appeared, and because she was clothed I hardly recognized her. A dress and high heels and lots of makeup. Big gold earrings. "Here I am!" she said gaily. "And here's his stuff."

She handed me a plaid dog coat that was covered with dust, and an old rubber mouse. "Here are his things," she said.

I tried to be polite as I took them. "Thanks a lot."

"Thank *you*, Heidi. I really mean that. You've solved a big problem for me."

MacGregor watched the exchange of his possessions from Mrs. Brown to me. And the look on his face was so resigned that it almost broke my heart. He sat there, looking at his coat and his mouse, and his tail gave one wag. Then it was still. "He doesn't understand what's happening," Mrs. Brown said cheerfully.

"Yes, he does," I said. "He knows exactly what's happening. First his master gave him to you, and now you give him to me. He wonders who will be next."

Mrs. Brown laughed. "Come on now, Heidi! You're *projecting*."

"So long," I said.

I walked the dogs home via Lexington Avenue, and at a pet store I stopped and bought MacGregor a dog bed. It was important that he have his own sleeping quarters, just as Happy had his. God, I prayed, please don't let Shirley be home.

She wasn't. She was at the beauty parlor or something, because the apartment was peaceful and still. I took off MacGregor's leash and patted him. "This is it, old boy. Your new home. Happy will show you around."

And that's just what Happy did. Trotting along in an official kind of way, he led MacGregor around the apartment—into Shirley's room, then mine, then the living room and dining room. He showed him the kitchen and the tiny maid's room. He showed him the den, where we sometimes watch TV. The look on MacGregor's face was guarded, but he trotted after Happy dutifully. He sniffed everything and investigated the hall closet. He eyed Happy's toys.

I gave them each a bowl of water and a few dog biscuits. Then I led them into my room, put MacGregor's bed alongside Happy's and said, "This is where you sleep." I wanted to laugh then, because each dog took possession of his own bed at once. Obviously, there would be no fooling around about beds.

Dragging the hall phone into my room, I dialed Lionel's number. "Hello?" he said promptly. "Moss speaking."

"Lionel, it's me. And I've got MacGregor. I didn't have to kidnap him! She gave him to me!"

"Oh!" said Lionel. "How wonderful."

"Isn't it? And I really think he'll be happy here. I got him his own bed and everything."

"I'm so thrilled for you, dearest."

And suddenly I knew that he *was* thrilled for me. Because who in the world but Lionel would be thrilled that I had acquired another dog? Not a college degree, not fame and fortune, but a dog. "Lionel . . ."

"I'll make him a present of a new leash. And perhaps a case of that special dog food called Woof. It's vitamin enriched."

Oh Lionel, I wanted to say, you really are a nice person. In fact, you're the only person who has ever tried to understand my passion for dogs. Jeffrey understood it in a way, but he and I knew each other briefly, so that makes you the first to understand. You probably *will* go out and buy MacGregor a case of Woof. You'll probably buy him toys.

"Where shall we dine tonight, beloved?" Lionel was asking.

"Let's have a picnic in the park. And then I can bring the dogs."

"Wonderful," said Lionel Moss. "I'll buy a small bottle of champagne."

17

"I don't believe this!" my mother was saying. "I don't believe what I see! How could you have taken in another dog? One was too much, so now we have two! And without asking me—that's what I can't understand. Without even asking my permission."

She was pacing back and forth across the living room. Happy, MacGregor and I sat on the couch, watching her.

"I'm not a difficult person. Nobody has ever thought I was difficult. I try to be fair. But this time, Heidi, you have gone too far."

"I'm keeping him," I said. "Sorry."

"But you didn't ask me!"

"If I'd asked you, you would have said no."

"But who *is* this dog? We know nothing about him."

"His name is MacGregor and he comes from Seventy-fourth Street. He was an abused dog and I rescued him."

"Abused? What do you mean, abused?"

"Well, not so much abused as neglected. His owner neglected him."

My mother stopped pacing the room and stared at MacGregor. He was watching her intently. "What kind of dog is he?"

"A Scottie. Purebred."

"I see."

"They cost a lot of money, you know. The puppies can cost as much as five hundred dollars."

"Five hundred? Is that what this dog cost?"

"Probably. And he really is purebred. I'll show you pictures of Scotties in my dog encyclopedia."

As though she was a balloon out of which the air had escaped, Shirley sank down near the window. "It's going to rain," she said.

It was odd, but for the moment she'd forgotten about MacGregor. Her mind seemed to be on something else. "Is anything wrong?" I asked.

"I don't know. I'm just tired, I guess."

"How's the doctor?" I said cautiously.

She was looking out of the window, drumming her fingers on the arm of her chair. "He's all right. We're eating Mexican this evening."

"Right."

"I don't know . . . sometimes I think the only thing

I'm getting out of this relationship is indigestion."

"Then why go on with it?"

She gave me a sharp look. "Love isn't everything, Heidi. When you're older, you'll understand."

It was two in the afternoon and she was all dressed up, in one of those silk dresses she likes, and heels, and her good jewelry. Her hair had just been done at the beauty parlor—a permanent—and her makeup was perfect. But she looked sad. "What's the doctor's place like on Long Island?" I asked. "Is it nice?"

She shrugged. "Nice, schmice, who knows. It's all done in *her* taste, so it's hard to tell."

I assumed that "her" was Dr. Eisenberg's first wife. "You mean it's garish?"

Shirley began to tap her foot, the way she always does when she's annoyed. "The woman obviously had no taste, that's all. I mean, she has garden furniture in the living room."

"Is that bad?"

"Bad? To use wrought-iron furniture in the living room? My God, Heidi, you know better than that. And the bar is done with blue mirrors. Awful."

In the silence that followed, I stared at Happy and MacGregor. They were asleep, side by side, on the couch. Finally Shirley said, "I met the son, you know. The nutritionist."

"No kidding? What's he like?"

"A nut," Shirley said flatly, "a weirdo. He gave

133

me a bottle of vitamin K. I had never heard of it before."

"Is he attractive?"

"No, I just told you, he's a nut. Bushy hair and crazy eyes. He works at a health clinic in Yonkers."

All of a sudden, I wanted to tell her about Lionel. I wanted to describe him, and tell her that he was in love with me, and ask her advice. I wanted to find out if deep down she really believed that "love isn't everything." And so, did I turn to her and unburden myself? Did I ask her to counsel me—mother to daughter? No. I talked about Howard the nutritionist, who works in Yonkers.

At seven that evening, I met Lionel in Central Park—and as I approached, with MacGregor and Happy in tow, I saw that he had spread out a white picnic cloth on the grass. He had brought silver too, and real plates, and linen napkins. For one moment, I heard my mother's voice telling me—from childhood onward—that those who sit in the Park at night are candidates for the morgue. Then I greeted Lionel. "How pretty this looks, Lionel. You thought of everything."

"Champagne!" he said, pointing to a wine cooler that held a tiny bottle of Moët & Chandon. "And presents, too."

There were two small presents sitting on the picnic cloth—wrapped in tissue paper. "But Lionel, it isn't anyone's birthday, is it?"

134

"The presents," Lionel announced, "are for the dogs."

With a flourish, he opened the bottle of Moët and poured us each a glass. We toasted one another and drank, as the dogs sat and watched. I couldn't get over how good Happy and MacGregor looked together—one black, one taffy colored.

It was a humid evening, with a sky the color of lilac. And it seemed doubtful that we would be murdered, as the Park was very crowded. People walked their dogs and kids rode bicycles. Men sat on park benches, reading newspapers. Somewhere in the dull, lilac-colored sky the sun was going down.

Lionel raised his glass to me. " 'We have found safety with all things undying.' "

"Brooke," I said. "A poem he wrote for Cathleen."

Lionel looked surprised. "My goodness, dearest, how could you remember that?"

"I remember everything you tell me, Lionel."

Which was true, in a way. Because no matter how boring it was, I tried to remember the literary things he told me. Emily Dickinson's relationship with her brother, and Tolstoy's battles with his wife. Flaubert's travels in Egypt. The young Colette acting in vaudeville.

I took a sip of my champagne. "Lionel—why do people really write poems? Do you know?"

The question did not faze him. "Of course I know,

darling. To write a poem is to strike a hand against death, to have one brief moment of immortality. To write a poem means that one will not 'go gentle into that good night.' "

"Dylan Thomas," I said.

Lionel smiled at me. "Would the dogs like to open their presents?"

I giggled. "I don't know. Why don't you ask them?"

Lionel handed each dog its present. Officiating as "Mother," I opened them.

He had bought each dog a new collar and leash. But, let me assure you, these were not ordinary leashes and collars—these were made of the softest, finest leather, and they came from England. Happy's set was green and MacGregor's was red.

"Oh, Lionel, how beautiful. But so expensive."

"No less than they deserve," said Lionel. "Let's try them on."

We put the new collars on the dogs, and then the leashes. They looked great. Raising his glass, Lionel said, "I would like to propose a toast to Happy and MacGregor. May they live long and have wonderful lives." He raised his glass and drank, and so did I.

He had brought us an elegant dinner from Zabar's—a fancy grocery over on the West Side. Poached fish and a salad, and rolls and butter. For dessert there were cherry tarts. I'm not much of a drinker, but I did enjoy the champagne. It was cold and dry.

As the sun went down, the lights of the city began to twinkle like jewels. Down on Central Park South the tall towers of apartment buildings flashed and shone. It was funny, but I could hear the music of the Park carousel, far away. The dogs were asleep on the grass. "Lionel . . ."

He looked at me in the dim light. "Yes, beloved?"

"MacGregor is a nice dog, isn't he?"

Lionel gazed at the sleeping MacGregor. "He's more than nice. He's distinguished."

And that's when I fell in love with him. With Lionel Moss. There were no trumpets or anything, no flashes of light. I just knew that I loved him very very much.

"How do you mean, distinguished?" I said in a small voice.

It was dark now, and I could just see the outlines of Lionel's face. "I don't know, dearest. It's just that certain dogs, like people, have character. MacGregor has got it, and so has Happy. You have it, too."

And so do you, I wanted to say. So do you.

I could barely see his face in the dim light. But his thick blond hair was gleaming, and his strong white fingers stood out in the darkness. How incredible he was—both masculine and sensitive. The first person I had ever met who combined those qualities. "The dinner was beautiful," I said.

137

He was leaning back on one elbow, humming to himself. He seemed content. But I wasn't, because all of a sudden I knew that I loved Lionel Moss and that I wanted to make out with him. Life had happened to me while I was making other plans.

I reached over and took his hand, and he did not draw away. Then, as delicately as I could, I kissed him on the cheek, near the corner of his mouth. He didn't protest, which was what I had expected. Instead, he kissed me back, somewhere near my left ear. His mouth was soft and warm.

He moved closer to me and took my face between his hands. Then, gently, deliberately, he kissed me on the mouth.

18

"Why do you look like that?" Rupert Brooke had written to Cathleen. "Have you any idea what you look like? I didn't know that human beings could look like that. It's as far beyond beauty as beauty is beyond ugliness."

I was sitting on Lionel's living room couch, reading *The Love Letters of Rupert Brooke* while Lionel was at the dentist. This particular letter had been written early in the romance with Cathleen. Poor kids, I thought, to be so deeply in love and then to be parted. To go unconsummated, as Lionel would say. What a shame. Lionel and I, on the other hand, were very close to consummation because we were making out at every conceivable moment. Not that either of us had lost our virginity yet, but I felt that the event was on the horizon. We kissed in the Park these days, and held hands in restaurants, and necked passionately in his apartment. He was such a good lover! And so gentle. He was born, as I told him one evening, to make love.

We would lie on his couch and kiss for hours—and the more I got to know him, the more I could NOT believe that he had never made out. But he hadn't. The only person he had dated steadily before me was a typist named Gloria who worked at the University of Virginia, in the dean's office. It was true. Lionel's only previous relationship was with a forty-year-old typist who was not pretty, but who did like poetry. They had dated for the whole of Lionel's senior year, and yet they had never had sex.

"Didn't that make her mad?" I had asked him, as we lay in each other's arms one afternoon.

"Well, yes," he mumbled into my hair. "In a way."

What way was that? I wanted to ask, but I didn't because Lionel was so very reticent about Gloria. Poor woman. It was clear that all she had wanted was a little affection.

However. With Lionel and me it was going to be different because our lovemaking was growing more and more intense. Mentally, I was preparing myself to send *the* telegram to my friend Veronica in Los Angeles. When she moved away we had agreed to wire one another if either of us lost her virginity. My own telegram, I decided, would be cryptic and to the point. Something like, "Gone with the wind. Love, Heidi."

I returned to Rupert's letters to Cathleen. "I'd say you were beautiful if the word weren't a million times too feeble," he had written. "My God! I adore you."

I tucked my legs under me on the couch and read onward. And it was then that the door to Lionel's apartment opened, and a woman walked in.

I almost fell off the couch—that's how startled I was. I mean, the door was unlocked, but I hadn't heard the knob turn. Quietly and stealthily, a woman with white hair stepped into the room and surveyed me. She was tall and chic and dressed in a beige linen suit. She was also Clemence Vale.

How could I not have recognized her? I had stared at her portrait in Lionel's living room a hundred times. He had showed me photos of her in old albums. The only thing was, she was better-looking than either the photos or the painting. With her beige suit, and silk scarf, and understated jewelry, she was what my mother would have called stunning.

"I'm so sorry," said the woman. "Did I startle you?"

I rose quickly to my feet. "No, ma'am. I mean, yes, you did. I'm a friend of Lionel's. He's at the dentist right now. I was just waiting for him."

A little smile crossed her face, and then it was

gone. I wondered what she was doing in New York. She was supposed to be in Virginia.

"Uh, won't you sit down?" I said. "Lionel should be back very soon. He's at the dentist."

"So you said," said Clemence Vale. She looked around the room carefully, and chose a straight-backed chair. "And you are . . ."

"Heidi Moss," I said. "I mean, Heidi Rosenbloom! I'm a friend of Lionel's."

How I wished, at that moment, that Happy and MacGregor were with me. I had left them home, and now I regretted it. They could have given me moral support.

"Heidi Rosenbloom?" the woman said, as though the words were slightly distasteful. "I don't think Lionel has mentioned you."

"No, ma'am," I said nervously.

"I'm his aunt. Aunt Clemence."

"Yes, ma'am. I recognized you from the portrait."

Her eyes flickered over the portrait that showed her sitting on a bench in a hunting costume—a Great Dane by her side. "It should have been a Beagle," I said. "Or maybe, a Foxhound."

"I beg your pardon?"

"In the picture. But of course, it doesn't matter."

"No," she said. "It doesn't."

"Does Lionel know you're in town? Does he expect you?"

Clemence Vale took out a cigarette and lit it. It

wasn't a normal cigarette, but one of those long black foreign-looking ones. I hurried into the kitchen to get her an ashtray.

"Thank you," she said, taking the ashtray. "No, Lionel doesn't know I'm in New York. But I had to come up for a few days to see my publisher, and so I thought it would be a good time for the Lion and I to talk. To work out a few problems."

"The Lion?"

"That's my pet name for Lionel. Just our little joke together."

"Oh," I said. "Right."

A silence descended on us, one of those silences that I hate, and so to fill the gap, I said, "I've read some of your books, Miss Vale. Uh, they're very interesting."

A tiny smile crossed her face. "You're a mystery fan?"

"No ma'am. I mean, not really. But I did read three of your books."

I had meant to compliment her in some way, but found that I couldn't do it. Because I didn't like her books—they were too violent.

She was gazing around the room, studying the books and the furniture, admiring her own portrait. "Have you been here before?" I asked.

She nodded. "Of course. The Lion is very neat, isn't he? Something my friend Cornelia taught him long ago."

"Yes, ma'am."

"Children are as messy as pigs, but she broke Lionel of that very early. When he failed to tidy his room, she would lock him in the attic."

"Really?"

"Yes," said Miss Vale with satisfaction, "she would lock him in the attic and there he would stay until he repented. Once he was there for two days. In the dark."

I felt a sinking sensation in my stomach, as though something terrible was about to happen—or be revealed—but I didn't know what to do about it.

"Well, he's very neat now," I said lamely. "He's a real perfectionist."

She smiled—that tiny, ungenerous smile. "Of course he is. That's the way we brought him up—to be neat, and silent, and obedient. To respect adults." Suddenly, she saw the ring on my left hand, the little sapphire surrounded by diamonds. "What are you doing with that ring?"

"Well . . ."

"That ring belonged to Lionel's mother!"

"Uh, yes ma'am, I know. But Lionel gave it to me. We're sort of engaged."

"Engaged!" she said, rising to her feet. "What on earth are you talking about? He's never mentioned you. How old are you?"

"I'm almost seventeen, and . . ."

"My God, I can't trust him for a minute. One

144

minute out of my sight, and he does this. I try to get to New York every month, to keep an eye on him, but a person can't be everywhere at once. I have my work, and a large house to manage, and a social life to maintain. It isn't easy to keep so many things in balance. But Lionel wanted to come here, and so I said all right. His own apartment, a teaching job . . . I agreed to everything. Just as long as he kept seeing Dr. Wilton three times a week. That was our bargain—see the psychiatrist, or no deal."

"The psychiatrist?"

Clemence Vale paused, as though she couldn't decide whether or not to trust me. She looked me up and down, and took a few puffs of her cigarette. "Dr. John Wilton is famous for treating people like Lionel, and his office happens to be on Park Avenue. So Lionel was allowed to move here, just as long as he worked with the doctor. Now, of course, it is evident that he's been lying. I mean, as far as you know, has he been having sessions?"

"I don't know. Really."

Miss Vale straightened her shoulders, like a general about to take charge of the troops. "Well, it's very clear that the whole thing hasn't worked out. I was here a month ago and he seemed to be all right—no crazy schemes, no delusions—but it's clear that he'll have to come home. He needs supervision."

"But . . . but he's twenty-three years old."

She laughed. "He is also quite mad."

I had been standing up, but now I sank back down on the couch. "I don't understand."

"Mad as a hatter. Always has been, always will be. But Dr. Wilton had him under control. At least, I thought he did. Oh, I could just kick myself for letting him live alone in a strange city. Engagement rings! But the doctor should have phoned me if anything was irregular."

Gathering my courage together in one small heap, I asked, "What's wrong with Lionel?"

"You don't know?" she said. "You mean, you're his friend and you don't know?" She went over to the bookcase, studied the books, and pulled one out. It was a slim volume of the poems of Rupert Brooke, but it was very old, with a cracked leather binding. *"This,"* she said, "is what's wrong with him."

As I opened the book, I saw that there was a photo of Rupert facing the title page. I had never seen him before, so I took a close look. Then I almost passed out. Because Rupert Brooke was the image of Lionel. I mean, the *image*. The beautiful face and the long blond hair. The classic nose. He even had a gold signet ring on his left hand.

"He has thought he was Rupert Brooke from the time he was fourteen," said Clemence Vale. "As a boy he begged me to send him to Rugby, in England, because Brooke had gone there. And later on, he began to fantasize that he had written Brooke's poems. Oh, I grant you that there's an uncanny resemblance, but is that enough to make a person go mad? So he looks like Rupert Brooke! So what! People tell me that *I* look like Glenda Jackson, the movie star, but do I let that drive me insane? Cornelia wanted to put him away somewhere, in an institution, but I refused to do that. I wanted to cure him, and I even took the risk of letting him teach in a prep school, here in New York. As far as I know, he's done pretty well at that—but his delusion hasn't changed. He still wears those white shirts and loosely knotted ties, still tries to be athletic, because Brooke was, and still tells me that he believes in chastity. Chastity! It's like something out of the Middle Ages."

She ground out her cigarette and turned away from me. And quickly, I realized two things. 1) that she had no intention of getting Lionel cured because 2) she liked him the way he was. Yep, Lionel's so-called craziness was just what she needed in life because it gave her power. And power—to this particular lady—was everything.

Miss Vale gave me her tight little smile. "You don't know what it was like to raise him. He used to cry by the hour, and refuse to eat, and hide under the covers with his books. Cornelia and I tried everything, all kinds of punishment, but nothing worked. From the age of fourteen, he insisted that he was Rupert Brooke."

"Lady," I said calmly, "if you were *my* aunt, I'd pretend to be Gertrude Stein."

Her mouth fell open in astonishment, but before she could reply, Lionel walked into the room. "Heidi, darling . . ." he began. And then he saw his aunt.

What happened next was amazing. Because all at once Lionel changed into a little boy—and Aunt Clemence changed into Florence Nightingale. She came over and embraced him, and he seemed to shrink before my eyes. He just seemed to get smaller and smaller, and younger and younger, as she hugged him. "It's my Lion," she said softly, "my beautiful Lion. He hasn't written Auntie for weeks."

"Oh, Auntie," said Lionel, burying his face in her shoulder. "What a surprise."

"The bad Lion didn't write Auntie, so she had to come all the way to New York," said Clemence, stroking Lionel's hair. "All the way to New York on a big airplane. And she brought him presents, just like she always does, and tonight she will take him out for a lovely din-din. Lions get so *very* hungry. Their aunties must feed them."

And it was then, dear friends, that I got out of there.

19

Four days later I sat on my bed, staring into space, as Happy and MacGregor played on the floor. That's right, they were playing, and if I hadn't been so emotionally devastated I would have enjoyed the sight. They were taking turns pouncing on MacGregor's rubber mouse—a game they had invented the other day. First one would worry the mouse while the other watched and growled. Then vice versa.

I couldn't get over what had happened. . . . Because just when I thought I had reality pinned down, it had gotten away from me. Yep, it had slithered away like a snake, making me wonder if anything was real at all. The day after I had left Lionel alone with his aunt, some flowers had been delivered to my building, a small bunch of carnations, and with them was a note. "Beloved, urgent business calls me

149

home to Virginia for a few weeks. Will you wait for me? And will you be faithful? I am always, believe me, your Lionel."

No, I had thought, you are not my Lionel—you are hers, and you won't be coming back. She's gotten you under her thumb again and she doesn't intend to let go. She will move you back into her house—now that Cornelia is no longer on the scene—and find you a new psychiatrist. You will sit there for the rest of your life, writing your thesis, and when you're bad she will lock you in the attic.

Happy had taken the mouse from MacGregor and was chewing on it. Enjoying the game, which was probably the first game of his life, MacGregor pretended to growl.

"OK," I said to the dogs, "so it's over. I'll pack up the ring and send it back to him, insured. I'll write a dignified note, saying good-bye. Because I am just no competition for Clemence Vale. And what's more, I do not care."

Not true. I did care. In fact, I cared so much that there were tears coming down my face. What a wild scenario. Auntie adopts small boy, and then proceeds to destroy him by alternating tenderness with cruelty. Auntie's girlfriend, platonic of course, is jealous so she tortures small boy, too. Small boy is sent to military school, where he suffers. Then to college, where the only person he feels secure enough to make out with is an aging typist. But by now, small boy is taking refuge in the fantasy that he is a poet who died in World War One. When he next falls in love, it is with a short Jewish teenager who dresses like a boy. . . . Miss Vale, I thought, you've missed quite a plot here. It's even more colorful than that corpse you placed on the bottom of an aquarium.

After a brief knock, my mother came into the room. She was wearing an old robe she uses to clean house in, and her hair was a mess. But the thing that I noticed was how pale she looked, how tired. She looked like she had been through a war.

"It's over," she said, standing in the doorway. "Finito. The end."

"What do you mean?" I said. "Come on in."

Stepping over the dogs, who were rolling around on the floor, she sat down on the wooden chair I had found on 73rd Street. "It's over. I ended it last night."

"The doctor, you mean?"

"Yes, the doctor. The friendly podiatrist. The gourmet. I just couldn't take it anymore, so it's over. Back to Wednesday matinées and bridge games with the girls."

"Do you want to talk about it?"

"There's nothing to talk about," she said angrily. "We're just not good together, that's all, and he *cannot* forget that first wife. Her picture is every-where. I mean, you go to the toilet, for God's sake, and there's a photograph of her."

"Well . . ."

"And he cries all the time, too. He starts talking about the first wife, and he cries. And then there's the son, the nut from Yonkers. It's all too much."

"Will you miss going out with him?"

"Miss it! Miss African food one night, and Korean the next? Miss that terrible house on the Island where the bar is done with blue mirrors, and the wife's photo is in the bathroom?"

But I could see that she would miss it, and that she was sorry to be unattached again. She would go back to her Wednesday matinées, and her card games, and her arguments with Leonard—and worst of all, she would go back to concentrating on me. On my hair and my figure and my clothes. On my future as the next Miss America.

"Ah, what's the use?" she said wearily. "I'm too set in my ways, and he's too set in his. Things will be different for you, baby. You're still young."

No, I'm not, I wanted to say to her. I'm not young at all. As a matter of fact, at this very moment I feel a hundred years old. Because my sense of reality has been so screwed up that I don't feel like trusting anyone again. A male, that is. And I no longer want to make out. Let everyone in my class lose their virginity—let them lose it en masse, in Times Square. It's back to the dogs for me, Mom. Back to the kennel.

"...a family conference," my mother was saying. "Because he's not going to accept it, Heidi."

"Who?" I said. "What?"

"I said that your father will not accept the idea of your not going to college. It would break his heart if you didn't go. So I want us to have a family conference about it next week. The three of us will go to lunch."

Restaurants, I thought. Our whole lives are being decided in restaurants.

"OK," I said, "we'll talk about it. But my mind is made up, you know."

Shirley shook her head. "Baby, what people think at sixteen is not what they think at thirty. You have a lot to learn."

20

It was September 16th, and I was sitting in the Park with Happy and MacGregor. Yesterday, I had turned seventeen. And in two more days school would start and I would be a senior. We were late starting this year because they were building a new wing onto the biology lab.

Everything was the same, and yet everything was different. I mean, my birthday dinner with my parents had been the usual disaster, with them giving me expensive presents I didn't want, and with the three of us getting into an argument. Leonard had been wild, really wild, about my not applying to college. And Shirley had wound up in tears. Which was par for the course. But something had changed during the past few weeks, and I could only assume that the something was me.

There was something different about me now, and while I didn't have words for it, I knew it was there. I felt it when I walked the nine dogs in the Park every day—Peter Applebaum wasn't back from Europe yet—and I felt it at night when I lay in a bubble bath and read Virginia Woolf. At least Lionel had done that much for me, at least he had made me more literate. And, once you got used to the language, *Orlando* wasn't boring at all. It was almost fun.

He never wrote me, you know—but I never expected him to. And my anger at him was gone. All I felt now was a kind of sadness that someone so sweet and good-looking should have fallen under the spell of a witch like Clemence Vale. Poor Lionel. He needed so much to be appreciated. He needed to be loved.

Don't we all? I thought, as I watched my two dogs. Happy was chewing on MacGregor's ear, and MacGregor seemed quite sanguine about it. Sanguine. Now there was a word I would never have known without Lionel Moss.

Had I really loved him? No. I had loved him for loving me—and when you came right down to it, that was a very crummy thing. And yet . . . maybe I had given Lionel some happiness during those weeks, and if so, then I was glad. I had loved being loved. Wow, I said to myself, how deluded you were.

"Well boys, it's just us now," I said to the dogs,

but they didn't look at me. They were too busy with their new friendship, too busy chewing on one another's ears.

Just us. Just Happy and MacGregor and me. But why not? Independence was the name of the game, and I had been crazy to think otherwise. In one more year I would be eighteen, and out on my own. In one more year I could do anything I liked—start my own dog-walking business, become a groomer, work for a vet.

It was a dull, hazy afternoon, and the Park looked different in the autumn light. I glanced up and saw my old friend the jogger passing, that cute boy with the twinkly eyes and turned-up nose. "Hi," he said as he passed—and then he hesitated, wondering perhaps if I was going to respond, if finally we were going to meet.

But all I said was, "Hi," and so he continued onward, glancing back over his shoulder to give me a grin, and then disappearing down the path.

There would be time for me to meet him, and there would even be time for me to like him. But not yet, I said to myself.

Not quite yet.